DYLAN THOMAS

A Visit to Grandpa's and Other Stories

DYLAN THOMAS

A Visit to Grandpa's and Other Stories

Drawings by Robin Jacques

J. M. Dent & Sons Ltd
London & Melbourne

First published 1984

Text copyright © the Trustees for the copyrights of
the late Dylan Thomas 1938, 1939, 1945, 1946

Illustrations copyright © Robin Jacques 1984

This book is set in 12/15 point VIP Sabon
by Inforum Ltd, Portsmouth
Printed in Great Britain by
Biddles Ltd, Guildford, for
J. M. Dent & Sons Ltd
Aldine House, 33 Welbeck Street, London W1M 8LX

British Library Cataloguing in Publication Data

Thomas, Dylan
    A visit to grandpa's.
    I. Title
    823'.914[J]   PZ7
    ISBN 0–460–06154–2

Contents

A Visit to Grandpa's 1

Extraordinary Little Cough 11

Quite Early One Morning 27

Holiday Memory 37

The Peaches 49

Who Do You Wish Was with Us? 73

The Fight 91

A Child's Christmas in Wales 109

A Visit to Grandpa's

In the middle of the night I woke from a dream full of whips and lariats as long as serpents, and runaway coaches on mountain passes, and wide, windy gallops over cactus fields, and I heard the man in the next room crying, 'Gee-up!' and 'Whoa!' and trotting his tongue on the roof of his mouth.

It was the first time I had stayed in grandpa's house. The floorboards had squeaked like mice as I climbed into bed, and the mice between the walls had creaked like wood as though another visitor was walking on them. It was a mild summer night, but curtains had flapped and branches beaten against the window. I had pulled the sheets over my head, and soon was roaring and riding in a book.

'Whoa there, my beauties!' cried grandpa. His voice sounded very young and loud, and his tongue had powerful hooves, and he made his bedroom into a great meadow. I thought I would see if he was ill, or had set his bedclothes on fire, for my mother had said that he lit his pipe under the blankets, and had warned me to run to his help if I smelt smoke in the night. I went on tiptoe through the darkness to his bedroom door, brushing against the furniture and upsetting a candlestick with a thump. When I saw there was a light in the room I felt

1

frightened, and as I opened the door I heard grandpa shout, 'Gee-up!' as loudly as a bull with a megaphone.

He was sitting straight up in bed and rocking from side to side as though the bed were on a rough road; the knotted edges of the counterpane were his reins; his invisible horse stood in a shadow beyond the bedside candle. Over a white flannel nightshirt he was wearing a red waistcoat with walnut-sized brass buttons. The over-filled bowl of his pipe smouldered among his whiskers like a little, burning hayrick on a stick. At the sight of me, his hands dropped from the reins and lay blue and quiet, the bed stopped still on a level road, he muffled his tongue into silence, and the horses drew softly up.

'Is there anything the matter, grandpa?' I asked, though the clothes were not on fire. His face in the candlelight looked like a ragged quilt pinned upright on the black air and patched all over with goat-beards.

He stared at me mildly. Then he blew down his pipe, scattering the sparks and making a high, wet dog-whistle of the stem, and shouted, 'Ask no questions.'

After a pause, he said slyly, 'Do you ever have nightmares, boy?'

I said, 'No.'

'Oh, yes, you do,' he said.

I said I was woken by a voice that was shouting to horses.

'What did I tell you?' he said. 'You eat too much. Who ever heard of horses in a bedroom?'

He fumbled under his pillow, brought out a small tinkling bag, and carefully untied its strings. He put a sovereign in my hand and said, 'Buy a cake.' I thanked him and wished him good night.

As I closed my bedroom door, I heard his voice crying loudly and gaily, 'Gee-up! Gee-up!' and the rocking of the travelling bed.

In the morning I woke from a dream of fiery horses on a plain that was littered with furniture, and of large, cloudy men who rode six horses at a time and whipped them with burning bedclothes. Grandpa was at breakfast, dressed in deep black. After breakfast he said, 'There was a terrible loud wind last night,' and sat in his arm-chair by the hearth to make clay balls for the fire. Later in the morning he took me for a walk, through Johnstown village and into the fields on the Llanstephan road.

A man with a whippet said, 'There's a nice morning, Mr. Thomas,' and when he had gone, leanly as his dog, into the short-treed green wood he should not have entered because of the notices, grandpa said, 'There, do you hear what he called you? Mister!'

We passed by small cottages, and all the men who leant on the gates congratulated grandpa on the fine morning. We passed through the wood full of pigeons, and their wings broke the branches as they rushed to the tops of the trees. Among the soft, contented voices and the loud, timid flying, grandpa said, like a man calling across a field, 'If you heard those old birds in the night, you'd wake me up and say there were horses in the trees.'

We walked back slowly, for he was tired, and the lean man stalked out of the forbidden wood with a rabbit held as gently over his arm as a girl's arm in a warm sleeve.

On the last day but one of my visit I was taken to Llanstephan in a governess cart pulled by a short, weak pony. Grandpa might have been driving a bison, so tightly he held the reins, so ferociously cracked the long whip, so blasphemously shouted warning to boys who played in the road, so stoutly stood with his gaitered legs apart and cursed the demon strength and wilfulness of his tottering pony.

'Look out, boy!' he cried when we came to each corner, and pulled and tugged and jerked and sweated and waved his whip like a rubber sword. And when the pony had crept miserably round each corner, grandpa turned to me with a sighing smile, 'We weathered that one, boy.'

When we came to Llanstephan village at the top of the hill, he left the cart by the 'Edwinsford Arms' and patted the pony's muzzle and gave it sugar, saying, 'You're a weak little pony, Jim, to pull big men like us.'

He had strong beer and I had lemonade, and he paid Mrs. Edwinsford with a sovereign out of the tinkling bag; she inquired after his health, and he said that Llangadock was better for the tubes. We went to look at the church-yard and the sea, and sat in the wood called the Sticks, and stood on the concert platform in the middle of the wood where visitors sang on midsummer nights and, year by year, the innocent of the village was elected mayor. Grandpa paused at the churchyard and pointed over the iron gate at the angelic headstones and the poor wooden crosses. 'There's no sense in lying there,' he said.

We journeyed back furiously: Jim was a bison again.

I woke late on my last morning, out of dreams where the Llanstephan sea carried bright sailing-boats as long as liners; and heavenly choirs in the Sticks, dressed in bards' robes and brass-buttoned waistcoats, sang in a strange Welsh to the departing sailors. Grandpa was not at breakfast; he rose early. I walked in the fields with a new

4

sling, and shot at the Towy gulls and the rooks in the parsonage trees. A warm wind blew from the summer points of the weather; a morning mist climbed from the ground and floated among the trees and hid the noisy birds; in the mist and the wind my pebbles flew lightly up like hailstones in a world on its head. The morning passed without a bird falling.

I broke my sling and returned for the midday meal through the parson's orchard. Once, grandpa told me, the parson had bought three ducks at Carmarthen Fair and made a pond for them in the centre of the garden, but they waddled to the gutter under the crumbling doorsteps of the house, and swam and quacked there. When I reached the end of the orchard path, I looked through a hole in the hedge and saw that the parson had made a tunnel through the rockery that was between the gutter and the pond and had set up a notice in plain writing, 'This way to the pond.'

The ducks were still swimming under the steps.

Grandpa was not in the cottage. I went into the garden, but grandpa was not staring at the fruit-trees. I called across to a man who leant on a spade in the field beyond the garden hedge, 'Have you seen my grandpa this morning?'

He did not stop digging, and answered over his shoulder, 'I seen him in his fancy waistcoat.'

Griff, the barber, lived in the next cottage. I called to him through the open door, 'Mr. Griff, have you seen my grandpa?'

The barber came out in his shirtsleeves.

I said, 'He's wearing his best waistcoat.' I did not know

if it was important, but grandpa wore his waistcoat only in the night.

'Has grandpa been to Llanstephan?' asked Mr. Griff anxiously.

'He went there yesterday in a little trap,' I said.

He hurried indoors and I heard him talking in Welsh, and he came out again with his white coat on, and he carried a striped and coloured walking-stick. He strode down the village street and I ran by his side.

When we stopped at the tailor's shop, he cried out, 'Dan!' and Dan Tailor stepped from his window where he sat like an Indian priest but wearing a derby hat. 'Dai Thomas has got his waistcoat on,' said Mr. Griff, 'and he's been to Llanstephan.'

As Dan Tailor searched for his overcoat, Mr. Griff was striding on. 'Will Evans,' he called outside the carpenter's shop, 'Dai Thomas has been to Llanstephan, and he's got his waistcoat on.'

'I'll tell Morgan now,' said the carpenter's wife out of the hammering, sawing darkness of the shop.

We called at the butcher's shop and Mr. Price's house, and Mr. Griff repeated his message like a town crier.

We gathered together in Johnstown square. Dan Tailor had his bicycle, Mr. Price his pony trap. Mr. Griff, the butcher, Morgan carpenter, and I climbed into the shaking trap, and we trotted off towards Carmarthen town. The tailor led the way, ringing his bell as though there were a fire or a robbery, and an old woman by the gate of a cottage at the end of the street ran inside like a pelted hen. Another woman waved a bright handkerchief.

'Where are we going?' I asked.

Grandpa's neighbours were as solemn as old men with black hats and jackets on the outskirts of a fair. Mr. Griff shook his head and mourned, 'I didn't expect this again from Dai Thomas.'

'Not after last time,' said Mr. Price sadly.

We trotted on, we crept up Constitution Hill, we rattled down into Lammas Street, and the tailor still rang his bell and a dog ran, squealing, in front of his wheels. As we clip-clopped over the cobbles that led down to the Towy bridge, I remembered grandpa's nightly noisy journeys that rocked the bed and shook the walls, and I saw his gay waistcoat in a vision and his patchwork head tufted and smiling in the candlelight. The tailor before us turned round on his saddle, his bicycle wobbled and skidded. 'I see Dai Thomas!' he cried.

The trap rattled on to the bridge, and I saw grandpa there: the buttons of his waistcoat shone in the sun, he wore his tight, black Sunday trousers and a tall, dusty hat I had seen in a cupboard in the attic, and he carried an ancient bag. He bowed to us. 'Good morning, Mr. Price,' he said, 'and Mr. Griff and Mr. Morgan and Mr. Evans.' To me he said, 'Good morning, boy.'

Mr. Griff pointed his coloured stick at him.

'And what do you think you are doing on Carmarthen bridge in the middle of the afternoon,' he said sternly, 'with your best waistcoat and your old hat?'

Grandpa did not answer, but inclined his face to the river wind, so that his beard was set dancing and wagging as though he talked, and watched the coracle men move, like turtles, on the shore.

Mr. Griff raised his stunted barber's pole. 'And where do you think you are going,' he said, 'with your black bag?'

Grandpa said, 'I am going to Llangadock to be buried.' And he watched the coracle shells slip into the water lightly, and the gulls complain over the fish-filled water as bitterly as Mr. Price complained,

'But you aren't dead yet, Dai Thomas.'

For a moment grandpa reflected, then, 'There's no sense in lying dead in Llanstephan,' he said. 'The ground is comfy in Llangadock; you can twitch your legs without putting them in the sea.'

His neighbours moved close to him. They said, 'You aren't dead, Mr. Thomas.'

'How can you be buried, then?'

'Nobody's going to bury you in Llanstephan.'

'Come on home, Mr. Thomas.'

'There's strong beer for tea.'

'And cake.'

But grandpa stood firmly on the bridge, and clutched his bag to his side, and stared at the flowing river and the sky, like a prophet who has no doubt.

Extraordinary Little Cough

One afternoon, in a particularly bright and glowing August, some years before I knew I was happy, George Hooping, whom we called Little Cough, Sidney Evans, Dan Davies, and I sat on the roof of a lorry travelling to the end of the Peninsula. It was a tall, six-wheeled lorry, from which we could spit on the roofs of the passing cars and throw our apple stumps at women on the pavement. One stump caught a man on a bicycle in the middle of the back, he swerved across the road, for a moment we sat quiet and George Hooping's face grew pale. And if the lorry runs him over, I thought calmly as the man on the bicycle swayed towards the hedge, he'll get killed and I'll be sick on my trousers and perhaps on Sidney's too, and we'll be arrested and hanged, except George Hooping who didn't have an apple.

But the lorry swept past; behind us, the bicycle drove into the hedge, the man stood up and waved his fist, and I waved my cap back at him.

'You shouldn't have waved your cap,' said Sidney Evans, 'he'll know what school we're in.' He was clever, dark, and careful, and had a purse and a wallet.

'We're not in school now.'

'Nobody can expel me,' said Dan Davies. He was leaving next term to serve in his father's fruit shop for a salary.

11

We all wore haversacks, except George Hooping whose mother had given him a brown-paper parcel that kept coming undone, and carried a suitcase each. I had placed a coat over my suitcase because the initials on it were 'N. T.' and everybody would know that it belonged to my sister. Inside the lorry were two tents, a box of food, a packing-case of kettles and saucepans and knives and forks, an oil lamp, a primus stove, ground sheets and blankets, a gramophone with three records, and a table-cloth from George Hooping's mother.

We were going to camp for a fortnight in Rhossilli, in a field above the sweeping five-mile beach. Sidney and Dan had stayed there last year, coming back brown and swearing, full of stories of campers' dances round the fires at midnight, and elderly girls from the training college who sun-bathed naked on ledges of rocks surrounded by laughing boys, and singing in bed that lasted until dawn. But George had never left home for more than a night; and then, he told me, one half-holiday when it was raining and there was nothing to do but stay in the wash-house racing his guineapigs giddily along the benches, it was only to stay in St. Thomas, three miles from his house, with an aunt who could see through the walls and who knew what a Mrs. Hoskin was doing in the kitchen.

'How much further?' asked George Hooping, clinging to his split parcel, trying in secret to push back socks and suspenders, enviously watching the solid green fields skim by as though the roof were a raft on an ocean with a motor in it. Anything upset his stomach, even liquorice and sherbet, but I alone knew that he wore long combinations in the summer with his name stitched in red on them.

'Miles and miles,' Dan said.

'Thousands of miles,' I said. 'It's Rhossilli, U.S.A. We're going to camp on a bit of rock that wobbles in the wind.'

'And we have to tie the rock on to a tree.'

'Cough can use his suspenders,' Sidney said.

The lorry roared round a space—'Upsy-daisy! Did you feel it then, Cough? It was on one wheel'—and below us, beyond fields and farms, the sea, with a steamer puffing on its far edge, shimmered.

'Do you see the sea down there, it's shimmering, Dan,' I said.

George Hooping pretended to forget the lurch of the slippery roof and, from that height, the frightening smallness of the sea. Gripping the rail of the roof, he said, 'My father saw a killer whale.' The conviction in his voice died quickly as he began. He beat against the wind with his cracked, treble voice, trying to make us believe. I knew he wanted to find a boast so big it would make our hair stand up and stop the wild lorry.

'Your father's a herbalist.' But the smoke on the horizon was the white, curling fountain the whale blew through his nose, and its black nose was the bow of the poking ship.

'Where did he keep it, Cough, in the wash-house?'

'He saw it in Madagascar. It had tusks as long as from here to, from here to . . .'

'From here to Madagascar.'

All at once the threat of a steep hill disturbed him. No longer bothered about the adventures of his father, a small, dusty, skullcapped and alpaca-coated man standing and mumbling all day in a shop full of herbs and curtained holes in the wall, where old men with backache and young girls in trouble waited for consultations in the half-dark, he stared at the hill swooping up and clung to Dan and me.

'She's doing fifty!'

'The brakes have gone, Cough!'

He twisted away from us, caught hard with both hands on the rail, pulled and trembled, pressed on a case behind him with his foot, and steered the lorry to safety round a stone-walled corner and up a gentler hill to a gate of a battered farm-house.

Leading down from the gate, there was a lane to the first beach. It was high tide, and we heard the sea dashing. Four boys on a roof—one tall, dark, regular-featured, precise of speech, in a good suit, a boy of the world; one squat, ungainly, red-haired, his red wrists fighting out of short, frayed sleeves; one heavily spectacled, small-paunched, with indoor shoulders and feet in always unlaced boots wanting to go different ways; one small, thin, indecisively active, quick to get dirty, curly—saw their field in front of them, a fortnight's new home that had thick, pricking hedges for walls, the sea for a front garden, a green gutter for a lavatory, and a wind-struck tree in the very middle.

I helped Dan unload the lorry while Sidney tipped the driver and George struggled with the farm-yard gate and looked at the ducks inside. The lorry drove away.

'Let's build our tents by the tree in the middle,' said George.

'Pitch!' Sidney said, unlatching the gate for him.

We pitched our tents in a corner, out of the wind.

'One of us must light the primus,' Sidney said, and, after George had burned his hand, we sat in a circle

14

outside the sleeping-tent talking about motor cars, content to be in the country, lazily easy in each other's company, thinking to ourselves as we talked, knowing always that the sea dashed on the rocks not far below us and rolled out into the world, and that tomorrow we would bathe and throw a ball on the sands and stone a bottle on a rock and perhaps meet three girls. The oldest would be for Sidney, the plainest for Dan, and the youngest for me. George broke his spectacles when he spoke to girls; he had to walk off, blind as a bat, and the next morning he would say, 'I'm sorry I had to leave you, but I remembered a message.'

It was past five o'clock. My father and mother would have finished tea; the plates with famous castles on them were cleared from the table; father with a newspaper, mother with socks, were far away in the blue haze to the left, up a hill, in a villa, hearing from the park the faint cries of children drift over the public tennis court, and wondering where I was and what I was doing. I was alone with my friends in a field, with a blade of grass in my mouth saying, 'Dempsey would hit him cold,' and thinking of the great whale that George's father never saw thrashing on the top of the sea, or plunging underneath, like a mountain.

'Bet you I can beat you to the end of the field.'

Dan and I raced among the cowpads, George thumping at our heels.

'Let's go down to the beach.'

Sidney led the way, running straight as a soldier in his khaki shorts, over a stile, down fields to another, into a wooded valley, up through heather on to a clearing near the edge of the cliff, where two broad boys were

wrestling outside a tent. I saw one bite the other in the leg, they both struck expertly and savagely at the face, one struggled clear, and, with a leap, the other had him face to the ground. They were Brazell and Skully.

'Hallo, Brazell and Skully!' said Dan.

Skully had Brazell's arm in a policeman's grip; he gave it two quick twists and stood up, smiling.

'Hallo, boys! Hallo, Little Cough! How's your father?'

'He's very well, thank you.'

Brazell, on the grass, felt for broken bones. 'Hallo, boys! How are your fathers?'

They were the worst and biggest boys in school. Every day for a term they caught me before class began and wedged me in the waste-paper basket and then put the basket on the master's desk. Sometimes I could get out and sometimes not. Brazell was lean, Skully was fat.

'We're camping in Button's field,' said Sidney.

'We're taking a rest cure here,' said Brazell. 'And how is Little Cough these days? Father given him a pill?'

We wanted to run down to the beach, Dan and Sidney and George and I, to be alone together, to walk and shout by the sea in the country, throw stones at the waves, remember adventures and make more to remember.

'We'll come down to the beach with you,' said Skully.

He linked arms with Brazell, and they strolled behind us, imitating George's wayward walk and slashing the grass with switches.

Dan said hopefully, 'Are you camping here for long, Brazell and Skully?'

'For a whole nice fortnight, Davies and Thomas and Evans and Hooping.'

When we reached Mewslade beach and flung ourselves down, as I scooped up sand and it trickled, grain by grain through my fingers, as George peered at the sea through his double lenses and Sidney and Dan heaped sand over his legs, Brazell and Skully sat behind us like two warders.

'We thought of going to Nice for a fortnight,' said Brazell—he rhymed it with ice, dug Skully in the ribs—'but the air's nicer here for the complexion.'

'It's as good as a herb,' said Skully.

They shared an enormous joke, cuffing and biting and wrestling again, scattering sand in the eyes, until they fell back with laughter, and Brazell wiped the blood from his nose with a piece of picnic paper. George lay covered to the waist in sand. I watched the sea slipping out, with birds quarrelling over it, and the sun beginning to go down patiently.

'Look at Little Cough,' said Brazell. 'Isn't he extraordinary? He's growing out of the sand. Little Cough hasn't got any legs.'

'Poor Little Cough,' said Skully, 'he's the most extraordinary boy in the world.'

'Extraordinary Little Cough,' they said together, 'extraordinary, extraordinary, extraordinary.' They made a song out of it, and both conducted with their switches.

'He can't swim.'

'He can't run.'

'He can't learn.'

'He can't bowl.'

'He can't bat.'

'And I bet he can't make water.'

George kicked the sand from his legs. 'Yes, I can!'

'Can you swim?'

'Can you run?'

'Can you bowl?'

'Leave him alone,' Dan said.

They shuffled nearer to us. The sea was racing out now. Brazell said in a serious voice, wagging his finger, 'Now, quite truthfully, Cough, aren't you extraordinary? Very extraordinary? Say "Yes" or "No".'

'Categorically, "Yes" or "No",' said Skully.

'No,' George said. 'I can swim and I can run and I can play cricket. I'm not frightened of anybody.'

I said, 'He was second in the form last term.'

'Now isn't that extraordinary? If he can be second he can be first. But no, that's too ordinary. Little Cough must be second.'

'The question is answered,' said Skully. 'Little Cough is extraordinary.' They began to sing again.

'He's a very good runner,' Dan said.

'Well, let him prove it. Skully and I ran the whole length of Rhossilli sands this morning, didn't we, Skull?'

'Every inch.'

'Can Little Cough do it?'

'Yes,' said George.

'Do it, then.'

'I don't want to.'

'Extraordinary Little Cough can't run,' they sang, 'can't run, can't run.'

Three girls, all fair, came down the cliff-side arm in arm, dressed in short, white trousers. Their arms and legs and throats were brown as berries; I could see when they laughed that their teeth were very white; they stepped on to the beach, and Brazell and Skully stopped singing.

Sidney smoothed his hair back, rose casually, put his hands in his pockets, and walked towards the girls, who now stood close together, gold and brown, admiring the sunset with little attention, patting their scarves, turning smiles on each other. He stood in front of them, grinned and saluted. 'Hallo, Gwyneth! Do you remember me?'

'La-di-da!' whispered Dan at my side, and made a mock salute to George still peering at the retreating sea.

'Well, if this isn't a surprise!' said the tallest girl. With little studied movements of her hands, as though she were distributing flowers, she introduced Peggy and Jean.

Fat Peggy, I thought, too jolly for me, with hockey legs and tomboy crop, was the girl for Dan; Sidney's Gwyneth was a distinguished piece and quite sixteen, as immaculate and unapproachable as a girl in Ben Evans' stores; but Jean, shy and curly, with butter-coloured hair, was mine. Dan and I walked slowly to the girls.

I made up two remarks, 'Fair's fair, Sidney, no bigamy abroad,' and 'Sorry we couldn't arrange to have the sea in when you came.'

Jean smiled, wriggling her heel in the sand, and I raised my cap.

'Hallo!'

The cap dropped at her feet.

As I bent down, three lumps of sugar fell from my blazer pocket. 'I've been feeding a horse,' I said, and began to blush guiltily when all the girls laughed.

I could have swept the ground with my cap, kissed my hand gaily, called them señoritas, and made them smile without tolerance. Or I could have stayed at a distance, and this would have been better still, my hair blown in the wind, though there was no wind at all that evening, wrapped in mystery and staring at the sun, too aloof to speak to girls; but I knew that all the time my ears would have been burning, my stomach would have been as hollow and as full of voices as a shell. 'Speak to them quickly, before they go away!' a voice would have said insistently over the dramatic silence, as I stood like Valentino on the edge of the bright, invisible bull-ring of the sands. 'Isn't it lovely here!' I said.

I spoke to Jean alone; and this is love, I thought, as she nodded her head and swung her curls and said, 'It's nicer than Porthcawl.'

Brazell and Skully were two big bullies in a nightmare; I forgot them when Jean and I walked up the cliff, and, looking back to see if they were baiting George again or wrestling together, I saw that George had disappeared around the corner of the rocks and that they were talking at the foot of the cliff with Sidney and the two girls.

'What's your name?'

I told her.

'That's Welsh,' she said.

'You've got a beautiful name.'

'Oh, it's just ordinary.'

'Shall I see you again?'

'If you want to.'

'I want to all right! We can go and bathe in the morning. And we can try to get an eagle's egg. Did you know that there were eagles here?'

'No,' she said. 'Who was that handsome boy on the beach, the tall one with dirty trousers?'

'He's not handsome, that's Brazell. He never washes or combs his hair or anything. He's a bully and he cheats.'

'I think he's handsome.'

22

We walked into Button's field, and I showed her inside the tents and gave her one of George's apples. 'I'd like a cigarette,' she said.

It was nearly dark when the others came. Brazell and Skully were with Gwyneth, one each side of her holding her arms, Sidney was with Peggy, and Dan walked, whistling, behind with his hands in his pockets.

'There's a pair,' said Brazell, 'they've been here all alone and they aren't even holding hands. You want a pill,' he said to me.

'Build Britain's babies,' said Skully.

'Go on!' Gwyneth said. She pushed him away from her, but she was laughing, and she said nothing when he put his arm around her waist.

'What about a bit of fire?' said Brazell.

Jean clapped her hands like an actress. Although I knew I loved her, I didn't like anything she said or did.

'Who's going to make it?'

'He's the best, I'm sure,' she said, pointing at me.

Dan and I collected sticks, and by the time it was quite dark there was a fire crackling. Inside the sleeping-tent, Brazell and Jean sat close together; her golden head was on his shoulder; Skully, near them, whispered to Gwyneth; Sidney unhappily held Peggy's hand.

'Did you ever see such a soppy lot?' I said, watching Jean smile in the fiery dark.

'Kiss me, Charley!' said Dan.

We sat by the fire in the corner of the field. The sea, far out, was still making a noise. We heard a few nightbirds. ' "Tu-whit! Tu-whoo!" Listen! I don't like owls,' Dan said, 'they scratch your eyes out!'——and tried not to listen to the soft voices in the tent. Gwyneth's laughter

23

floated out over the suddenly moonlit field, but Jean, with the beast, was smiling and silent in the covered warmth; I knew her little hand was in Brazell's hand.

'Women!' I said.

Dan spat in the fire.

We were old and alone, sitting beyond desire in the middle of the night, when George appeared, like a ghost, in the firelight and stood there trembling until I said, 'Where've you been? You've been gone hours. Why are you trembling like that?'

Brazell and Skully poked their heads out.

'Hallo, Cough my boy! How's your father? What have you been up to tonight?'

George Hooping could hardly stand. I put my hand on his shoulder to steady him, but he pushed it away.

'I've been running on Rhossilli sands! I ran every bit of it! You said I couldn't, and I did! I've been running and running!'

Someone inside the tent had put a record on the gramophone. It was a selection from *No, No, Nanette*.

'You've been running all the time in the dark, Little Cough?'

'And I bet I ran it quicker than you did, too!' George said.

'I bet you did,' said Brazell.

'Do you think we'd run five miles?' said Skully.

Now the tune was *Tea for Two*.

'Did you ever hear anything so extraordinary? I told you Cough was extraordinary. Little Cough's been running all night.'

'Extraordinary, extraordinary, extraordinary Little Cough,' they said.

Laughing from the shelter of the tent into the darkness, they looked like a boy with two heads. And when I stared round at George again he was lying on his back fast asleep in the deep grass and his hair was touching the flames.

Quite Early One Morning

Quite early one morning in the winter in Wales, by
the sea that was lying down still and green as
grass after a night of tar-black howling and rolling, I
went out of the house, where I had come to stay for a
cold unseasonable holiday, to see if it was raining still, if
the outhouse had been blown away, potatoes, shears,
rat-killer, shrimp-nets, and tins of rusty nails aloft in the
wind, and if all the cliffs were left. It had been such a
ferocious night that someone in the smoky shipped-
pictured bar had said he could feel his tombstone shaking
even though he was not dead, or at least was moving; but
the morning shone as clear and calm as one always
imagines tomorrow will shine.

The sun lit the sea town, not as a whole—from topmost
down—reproving zinc-roofed chapel to empty but for rats
and whispers grey warehouse on the harbour, but in
separate bright pieces. There, the quay shouldering out,
nobody on it now but the gulls and the capstans like
small men in tubular trousers. Here, the roof of the
police-station, black as a helmet, dry as a summons,
sober as Sunday. There, the splashed church, with a cloud
in the shape of a bell poised above it, ready to drift and
ring. Here the chimneys of the pink-washed pub, the pub

27

that was waiting for Saturday night as an over-jolly girl waits for sailors.

The town was not yet awake. The milkman lay still lost in the clangour and music of his Welsh-spoken dreams, the wish-fulfilled tenor voices more powerful than Caruso's, sweeter than Ben Davies's, thrilling past Cloth Hall and Manchester House up to the frosty hills. The town was not yet awake. Babies in upper bedrooms of salt-white houses dangling over water, or of bow-windowed villas squatting prim in neatly treed but unsteady hill streets, worried the light with their half in sleep cries. Miscellaneous retired sea captains emerged for a second from deeper waves than ever tossed their boats, then drowned again, going down down into a perhaps Mediterranean-blue cabin of sleep, rocked to the sea-beat of their ears. Landladies, shawled and bloused and aproned with sleep in the curtained, bombasined black of their once spare rooms, remember their loves, their bills, their visitors—dead, decamped, or buried in English deserts till the trumpet of next expensive August roused them again to the world of holiday rain, dismal cliff and sand seen through the weeping windows of front parlours, tasselled table-cloths, stuffed pheasants, ferns in pots, fading photographs of the bearded and censorious dead, autograph albums with a lock of limp and colourless beribboned hair lolling out between the thick black boards.

The town was not yet awake. Birds sang in eaves, bushes, trees, on telegraph wires, rails, fences, spars, and wet masts, not for love or joy, but to keep the other birds away. The landlords in feathers disputed the right of even the flying light to descend and perch.

The town was not yet awake, and I walked through the streets like a stranger come out of the sea, shrugging off weed and wave and darkness with each step, or like an inquisitive shadow, determined to miss nothing—not the preliminary tremor in the throat of the dawn-saying cock or the first whirring nudge of arranged time in the belly of the alarm clock on the trinketed chest of drawers under the knitted text and the done-by-hand water-colours of Porthcawl or Trinidad.

I walked past the small sea-spying windows, behind whose trim curtains lay mild-mannered men and women not yet awake and, for all I could know, terrible and violent in their dreams. In the head of Miss Hughes, 'The Cosy,' clashed the cymbals of an eastern court. Eunuchs struck gongs the size of Bethesda Chapel. Sultans with voices fiercer than visiting preachers demanded a most un-Welsh dance. Everywhere there glowed and rayed the colours of the small, slate-grey woman's dreams, purple, magenta, ruby, sapphire, emerald, vermilion, honey. But I could not believe it. She knitted in her tidy sleep-world a beige woollen shroud with 'Thou Shalt Not' on the bosom.

I could not imagine Cadwallader Davies the grocer in his near-to-waking dream, riding on horse-back, two-gunned and Cody-bold, through the cactus prairies. He added, he subtracted, he receipted, he filed a prodigious account with a candle dipped in dried egg.

What big seas of dreams ran in the Captain's sleep? Over what blue-whaled waves did he sail through a rainbow hail of flying-fishes to the music of Circe's swinish island? Do not let him be dreaming of dividends and bottled beer and onions.

29

Someone was snoring in one house. I counted ten savage and indignant grunts and groans like those of a pig in a model and mudless farm which ended with a window rattler, a wash-basin shaker, a trembler of tooth glasses, a waker of dormice. It thundered with me to the chapel railings, then brassily vanished.

The chapel stood grim and grey, telling the day there was to be no nonsense. The chapel was not asleep, it never cat-napped nor nodded nor closed its long cold eye. I left it telling the morning off and the sea-gull hung rebuked above it.

And climbing down again and up out of the town I heard the cocks crow from hidden farm-yards, from old roosts above waves where fabulous sea-birds might sit and cry, 'Neptune!' And a far-away clock struck from another church in another village in another universe, though the wind blew the time away. And I walked in the timeless morning past a row of white cottages almost expecting that an ancient man with a great beard and an hour-glass and a scythe under his night-dressed arm might lean from the window and ask me the time. I would have told him, 'Arise old counter of the heartbeats of albatrosses, and wake the cavernous sleepers of the town to a dazzling new morning.' I would have told him, 'You unbelievable Father of Eva and Dai Adam, come out, old chicken, and stir up the winter morning with your spoon of a scythe.' I would have told him—I would have scampered like a scalded ghost over the cliffs and down to the bilingual sea.

Who lived in these cottages? I was a stranger to the sea town, fresh or stale from the city where I worked for my bread and butter wishing it were laver-bread and country salty butter yolk-yellow. Fishermen certainly; no painters but of boats; no man-dressed women with shooting-sticks and sketch-books and voices like macaws to paint the reluctant heads of critical and sturdy natives who posed by the pint against the chapel-dark sea which would be made more blue than the bay of Naples—though shallower.

I walked on to the cliff path again, the town behind and below waking up now so very slowly; I stopped and turned and looked. Smoke from one chimney—the cobbler's I thought, but from that distance it may have been the chimney of the retired male nurse who had come to live in Wales after many years' successful wrestling with the mad rich of southern England. He was not liked. He measured you for a strait-jacket carefully with his eye; he saw you bounce from rubber walls like a sorbo ball. No behaviour surprised him. Many people of the town found it hard to resist leering at him suddenly around the corner, or convulsively dancing, or pointing with laughter and devilish good humour at invisible dog-fights merely to prove to him that they were normal.

Smoke from another chimney now. They were burning their last night's dreams. Up from a chimney came a long-haired wraith like an old politician. Someone had been dreaming of the Liberal Party. But no, the smoky figure wove, attenuated into a refined and precise grey comma. Someone had been dreaming of reading Charles Morgan. Oh! The town was waking now and I heard distinctly insistent over the slow-speaking sea the voices of the town blown up to me. And some of the voices said,

I am Miss May Hughes, 'The Cosy,' a lonely lady,
Waiting in her house by the nasty sea,
Waiting for her husband and pretty baby
To come home at last from wherever they may be.

I am Captain Tiny Evans, my ship was the *Kidwelly*,
And Mrs Tiny Evans has been dead for many a year.
'Poor Captain Tiny all alone,' the neighbours whisper,
But I like it all alone and I hated her.

Clara Tawe Jenkins, 'Madam' they call me,
An old contralto with her dressing-gown on,
And I sit at the window and I sing to the sea,
For the sea does not notice that my voice has gone.

Parchedig Thomas Evans making morning tea,
Very weak tea, too, you mustn't waste a leaf.
Every morning making tea in my house by the sea,
I am troubled by one thing only, and that, belief.

Open the curtains, light the fire, what are servants for?
I am Mrs. Ogmore Pritchard and I want another snooze.
Dust the china, feed the canary, sweep the drawing-room
    floor;
And before you let the sun in, mind he wipes his shoes.

I am only Mr. Griffiths, very short-sighted, B.A., Aber.
As soon as I finish my egg I must shuffle off to school.
O patron saint of teachers, teach me to keep order,
And forget those words on the blackboard—'Griffiths Bat
    is a fool.'

Do you hear that whistling?—It's me, I am Phoebe,
The maid at the King's Head, and I am whistling like a bird.
Someone spilt a tin of pepper in the tea.
There's twenty for breakfast and I'm not going to say a word.

Thus some of the voices of a cliff-perched town at the far
end of Wales moved out of sleep and darkness into the
new-born, ancient, and ageless morning, moved and were
lost.

Holiday Memory

August Bank Holiday. A tune on an ice-cream cornet. A slap of sea and a tickle of sand. A fanfare of sunshades opening. A wince and whinny of bathers dancing into deceptive water. A tuck of dresses. A rolling of trousers. A compromise of paddlers. A sunburn of girls and a lark of boys. A silent hullabaloo of balloons.

I remember the sea telling lies in a shell held to my ear for a whole harmonious, hollow minute by a small, wet girl in an enormous bathing-suit marked 'Corporation Property.'

I remember sharing the last of my moist buns with a boy and a lion. Tawny and savage, with cruel nails and capacious mouth, the little boy tore and devoured. Wild as seed-cake, ferocious as a hearth-rug, the depressed and verminous lion nibbled like a mouse at his half a bun, and hiccupped in the sad dusk of his cage.

I remember a man like an alderman or a bailiff, bowlered and collarless, with a bag of monkey-nuts in his hand, crying, 'Ride 'em, cowboy!' time and again as he whirled in his chairoplane giddily above the upturned laughing faces of the town girls bold as brass and the boys with padded shoulders and shoes sharp as knives; and the monkey-nuts flew through the air like salty hail.

Children all day capered or squealed by the glazed or

bashing sea, and the steam-organ wheezed its waltzes in the threadbare playground and waste lot, where the dodgems dodged, behind the pickle factory.

And mothers loudly warned their proud pink daughters or sons to put that jellyfish down; and fathers spread newspapers over their faces; and sand-fleas hopped on the picnic lettuce; and someone had forgotten the salt.

In those always radiant, rainless, lazily rowdy and sky-blue summers departed, I remember August Monday from the rising of the sun over the stained and royal town to the husky hushing of the roundabout music and the dowsing of the naphtha jets in the seaside fair: from bubble-and-squeak to the last of the sandy sandwiches.

There was no need, that holiday morning, for the sluggardly boys to be shouted down to breakfast; out of their jumbled beds they tumbled, scrambled into their rumpled clothes; quickly at the bath-room basin they catlicked their hands and faces, but never forgot to run the water loud and long as though they washed like colliers; in front of the cracked looking-glass bordered with cigarette-cards, in their treasure-trove bedrooms, they whisked a gap-tooth comb through their surly hair; and with shining cheeks and noses and tide-marked necks, they took the stairs three at a time.

But for all their scramble and scamper, clamour on the landing, catlick and toothbrush flick, hair-whisk and stair-jump, their sisters were always there before them. Up with the lady lark, they had prinked and frizzed and hot-ironed; and smug in their blossoming dresses, rib-boned for the sun, in gym-shoes white as the blanco'd snow, neat and silly with doilies and tomatoes they helped in the higgledy kitchen. They were calm; they were virtuous; they had washed their necks; they did not romp, or fidget; and only the smallest sister put out her tongue at the noisy boys.

And the woman who lived next door came into the kitchen and said that her mother, an ancient uncertain body who wore a hat with cherries, was having 'one of her days' and had insisted, that very holiday morning, in carrying all the way to the tram-stop a photograph album and the cut-glass fruit bowl from the front room.

This was the morning when father, mending one hole in the thermos-flask, made three; when the sun declared war on the butter, and the butter ran; when dogs, with all the sweet-binned backyards to wag and sniff and bicker in, chased their tails in the jostling kitchen, worried sandshoes, snapped at flies, writhed between legs, scratched among towels, sat smiling on hampers.

And if you could have listened at some of the open doors of some of the houses in the street you might have heard,

'Uncle Owen says he can't find the bottle-opener . . .'

'Has he looked under the hall-stand?'

'Willy's cut his finger . . .'

'Got your spade?'

'If somebody doesn't kill that dog . . .'

'Uncle Owen says why should the bottle-opener be under the hall-stand?'

'Never again, never again . . .'

'I know I put the pepper somewhere . . .'

'Willy's bleeding . . .'

'Look, there's a bootlace in my bucket . . .'

'Oh come *on*, come on . . .'

'Let's have a look at the bootlace in your bucket . . .'

'If I lay my hands on that dog . . .'

'Uncle Owen's found the bottle-opener ...'

'Willy's bleeding over the cheese ...'

And the trams that hissed like ganders took us all to the beautiful beach.

There was cricket on the sand, and sand in the sponge cake, sand-flies in the watercress, and foolish, mulish, religious donkeys on the unwilling trot. Girls undressed in slipping tents of propriety; under invisible umbrellas, stout ladies dressed for the male and immoral sea. Little naked navvies dug canals; children with spades and no ambition built fleeting castles; wispy young men, outside the bathing-huts, whistled at substantial young women and dogs who desired thrown stones more than the bones of elephants. Recalcitrant uncles huddled over luke ale in the tiger-striped marquees. Mothers in black, like wobbling mountains, gasped under the discarded dresses of daughters who shrilly braved the goblin waves. And fathers, in the once-a-year sun, took fifty winks. Oh, think of all the fifty winks along the paper-bagged sand.

Liquorice allsorts, and Welsh hearts, were melting, and the sticks of rock, that we all sucked, were like barbers' poles made of rhubarb.

In the distance, surrounded by disappointed theoreticians and an ironmonger with a drum, a cross man on an orange-box shouted that holidays were wrong.

And the waves rolled in, with rubber ducks and clerks upon them.

I remember the patient, laborious, and enamouring hobby, or profession, of burying relatives in sand.

I remember the princely pastime of pouring sand, from cupped hands or buckets, down collars and tops of dresses; the shriek, the shake, the slap.

I can remember the boy by himself, the beachcombing

lone-wolf, hungrily waiting at the edge of family cricket; the friendless fielder, the boy uninvited to bat or to tea.

I remember the smell of sea and seaweed, wet flesh, wet hair, wet bathing-dresses, the warm smell as of a rabbity field after rain, the smell of pop and splashed sunshades and toffee, the stable-and-straw smell of hot, tossed, tumbled, dug, and trodden sand, the swill-and-gaslamp smell of Saturday night, though the sun shone strong, from the bellying beer-tents, the smell of the vinegar on shelled cockles, winkle-smell, shrimp-smell, the dripping-oily backstreet winter-smell of chips in newspapers, the smell of ships from the sun-dazed docks round the corner of the sand-hills, the smell of the known and paddled-in sea moving, full of the drowned and herrings, out and away and beyond and further still towards the antipodes that hung their koala-bears and Maoris, kangaroos, and boomerangs, upside down over the backs of the stars.

And the noise of pummelling Punch, and Judy falling, and a clock tolling or telling no time in the tenantless town; now and again a bell from a lost tower or a train on the lines behind us clearing its throat, and always the hopeless, ravenous swearing and pleading of the gulls, donkey-bray and hawker-cry, harmonicas and toy trumpets, shouting and laughing and singing, hooting of tugs and tramps, the clip of the chair-attendant's puncher, the motor-boat coughing in the bay, and the same hymn and washing of the sea that was heard in the Bible.

'If it could only just, if it could only just?' your lips said again and again as you scooped, in the hob-hot sand, dungeons, garages, torture-chambers, train tunnels, arsenals, hangars for zeppelins, witches' kitchens, vam-

42

pires' parlours, smugglers' cellars, trolls' grog-shops, sewers, under a ponderous and cracking castle. 'If it could only just be like this for ever and ever amen.' August Monday all over the earth, from Mumbles where the aunties grew like ladies on a seaside tree to brown, bear-hugging Henty-land and the turtled Ballantyne Islands.

'Could donkeys go on ice?'

'Only if they got snowshoes.'

We snowshoed a meek, complaining donkey and galloped him off in the wake of the ten-foot-tall and Atlas-muscled Mounties, rifled and pemmicanned, who always, in the white gold rush wastes, got their black-oathed-and-bearded man.

'Are there donkeys on desert islands?'

'Only sort-of donkeys.'

'What d'you mean, sort-of donkeys?'

'Native donkeys. They hunt things on them!'

'Sort-of walruses and seals and things?'

'Donkeys can't swim!'

'These donkeys can. They swim like whales, they swim like anything, they swim like—'

'Liar.'

'Liar yourself.'

And two small boys fought fiercely and silently in the sand, rolling together in a ball of legs and bottoms.

Then they went and saw the pierrots, or bought vanilla ices.

Lolling or larrikin that unsoiled, boiling beauty of a common day, great gods with their braces over their vests sang, spat pips, puffed smoke at wasps, gulped and ogled, forgot the rent, embraced, posed for the dickybird, were coarse, had rainbow-coloured armpits, winked, belched, blamed the radishes, looked at Ilfracombe, played hymns on paper-and-comb, peeled bananas, scratched, found seaweed in their panamas, blew up paper bags and banged them, wished for nothing.

But over all the beautiful beach I remember most the children playing, boys and girls tumbling, moving jewels, who might never be happy again. And 'happy as a sandboy' is true as the heat of the sun.

Dusk came down; or grew up out of the sands and the sea; or curled around us from the calling docks and the bloodily smoking sun. The day was done, the sands brushed and ruffled suddenly with a sea-broom of cold wind.

And we gathered together all the spades and buckets and towels, empty hampers and bottles, umbrellas and fish-frails, bats and balls and knitting, and went—oh, listen, Dad!—to the fair in the dusk on the bald seaside field.

Fairs were no good in the day; then they were shoddy and tired; the voices of hoop-la girls were crimped as elocutionists; no cannon-ball could shake the roosting coconuts; the gondolas mechanically repeated their sober lurch; the Wall of Death was safe as a governess cart; the wooden animals were waiting for the night.

But in the night, the hoop-la girls, like operatic crows, croaked at the coming moon; whizz, whirl, and ten for a tanner, the coconuts rained from their sawdust like grouse from the Highland sky; tipsy the griffin-prowed gondolas weaved on dizzy rails and the Wall of Death was a spinning rim of ruin, and the neighing wooden horses took, to a haunting hunting tune, a thousand

Becher's Brooks as easily and breezily as hooved swallows.

Approaching, at dusk, the fair-field from the beach, we scorched and gritty boys heard above the belabouring of the batherless sea the siren voices of the raucous, horsy barkers.

'Roll up, roll up!'

In her tent and her rolls of flesh the Fattest Woman in the World sat sewing her winter frock, another tent, and fixed her little eyes, blackcurrants in blancmange, on the skeletons who filed and sniggered by.

'Roll up, roll up, roll up to see the Largest Rat on Earth, the Rover or Bonzo of vermin.'

Here scampered the smallest pony, like a Shetland shrew. And here 'The Most Intelligent Fleas', trained, reined, bridled, and bitted, minutely cavorted in their glass corral.

Round galleries and shies and stalls, pennies were burning holes in a hundred pockets.

Pale young men with larded hair and Valentino-black side-whiskers, fags stuck to their lower lips, squinted along their swivel-sighted rifles and aimed at ping-pong balls dancing on fountains.

In knife-creased, silver-grey, skirt-like Oxford bags, and a sleeveless, scarlet, zip-fastened shirt with yellow horizontal stripes, a collier at the strength-machine spat on his hands, raised the hammer, and brought it Thor-ing down. The bell rang for Blaina.

Outside his booth stood a bitten-eared and barndoor-chested pug with a nose like a twisted swede and hair that started from his eyebrows and three teeth yellow as a camel's inviting any sportsman to a sudden and sickening

basting in the sandy ring or a quid if he lasted a round; and, wiry, cocky, bow-legged, coal-scarred, boozed, sportsmen by the dozen strutted in and reeled out; and still those three teeth remained, chipped and camel-yellow in the bored, teak face.

Draggled and stout-wanting mothers, with haphazard hats, hostile hatpins, buns awry, bursting bags, and children at their skirts like pop-filled and jam-smeared limpets, screamed before distorting mirrors, at their suddenly tapering or tubular bodies and huge ballooning heads, and the children gaily bellowed at their own reflected bogies withering and bulging in the glass.

Old men, smelling of Milford Haven in the rain, shuffled, badgering and cadging, round the edges of the swaggering crowd, their only wares a handful of damp confetti.

A daring dash of schoolboys, safely, shoulder to shoulder, with their father's trilbies cocked at a desperate angle over one eye, winked at and whistled after the procession past the swings of two girls arm-in-arm: always one pert and pretty, and always one with glasses.

Girls in skulled and cross-boned tunnels shrieked, and were comforted.

Young men, heroic after pints, stood up on the flying chairoplanes, tousled, crimson, and against the rules.

Jaunty girls gave sailors sauce.

All the fun of the fair in the hot, bubbling night. The Man in the sand-yellow Moon over the hurdy of gurdies. The swing-boats swimming to and fro like slices of the moon. Dragons and hippogriffs at the prows of the gondolas breathing fire and Sousa. Midnight roundabout riders tantivying under the fairy-lights, huntsmen on billygoats and zebras hallooing under a circle of glow-worms.

And as we climbed home, up the gas-lit hill, to the still homes over the mumbling bay, we heard the music die and the voices drift like sand. And we saw the lights of the fair fade. And, at the far end of the seaside field, they lit their lamps, one by one, in the caravans.

The Peaches

The grass-green cart, with 'J. Jones, Gorsehill' painted
shakily on it, stopped in the cobblestone passage
between 'The Hare's Foot' and 'The Pure Drop'. It was
late on an April evening. Uncle Jim, in his black market
suit with a stiff white shirt and no collar, loud new boots,
and a plaid cap, creaked and climbed down. He dragged
out a thick wicker basket from a heap of straw in the
corner of the cart and swung it over his shoulder. I heard
a squeal from the basket and saw the tip of a pink tail
curling out as Uncle Jim opened the public door of 'The
Pure Drop'.

'I won't be two minutes,' he said to me. The bar was
full; two fat women in bright dresses sat near the door,
one with a small dark child on her knee; they saw Uncle
Jim and nudged up on the bench.

'I'll be out straight away,' he said fiercely, as though I
had contradicted him, 'you stay there quiet.'

The woman without the child raised up her hands.
'Oh, Mr. Jones,' she said in a high laughing voice. She
shook like a jelly.

Then the door closed and the voices were muffled.

I sat alone on the shaft of the cart in the narrow
passage, staring through a side window of 'The Hare's
Foot'. A stained blind was drawn half over it. I could see

into half of a smoky, secret room, where four men were playing cards. One man was huge and swarthy, with a handlebar moustache and a love-curl on his forehead; seated by his side was a thin, bald, pale old man with his cheeks in his mouth; the faces of the other two were in shadow. They all drank out of brown pint tankards and never spoke, laying the cards down with a smack, scraping at their match-boxes, puffing at their pipes, swallowing unhappily, ringing the brass bell, ordering more, by a sign of the fingers, from a sour woman with a flowered blouse and a man's cap.

The passage grew dark too suddenly, the walls crowded in, and the roofs crouched down. To me, staring timidly there in the dark passage in a strange town, the swarthy man appeared like a giant in a cage surrounded by clouds, and the bald old man withered into a black hump with a white top; two white hands darted out of the corner with invisible cards. A man with spring-heeled boots and a two-edged knife might be bouncing towards me from Union Street.

I called, 'Uncle Jim, Uncle Jim,' softly so that he should not hear.

I began to whistle between my teeth, but when I stopped I thought the sound went hissing on behind me. I climbed down from the shaft and stepped close to the half-blind window; a hand clawed up the pane to the tassel of the blind; in the little, packed space between me on the cobbles and the card-players at the table, I could not tell which side of the glass was the hand that dragged the blind down slowly. I was cut from the night by a stained square. A story I had made in the warm, safe island of my bed, with sleepy midnight Swansea flowing and rolling round outside the house, came blowing down to me then with a noise on the cobbles. I remembered the demon in the story, with his wings and hooks, who clung like a bat to my hair as I battled up and down Wales after a tall, wise, golden, royal girl from Swansea convent. I tried to remember her true name, her proper, long, black-stockinged legs, her giggle and paper curls, but the hooked wings tore at me and the colour of her hair and eyes faded and vanished like the grass-green of the cart that was a dark, grey mountain now standing between the passage walls.

And all this time the old, broad, patient, nameless mare stood without stirring, not stamping once on the cobbles or shaking her reins. I called her a good girl and stood on tiptoe to try to stroke her ears as the door of 'The Pure Drop' swung open and the warm lamplight from the bar dazzled me and burned my story up. I felt frightened no longer, only angry and hungry. The two fat women near the door giggled, 'Good night, Mr. Jones,' out of the rich noise and the comfortable smells. The child lay curled asleep under the bench. Uncle Jim kissed the two women on the lips.

'Good night.'

'Good night.'

'Good night.'

Then the passage was dark again.

He backed the mare into Union Street, lurching against her side, cursing her patience and patting her nose, and we both climbed into the cart.

'There are too many drunken gipsies,' he said as we rolled and rattled through the flickering lamp-lit town.

He sang hymns all the way to Gorsehill in an affectionate bass voice, and conducted the wind with his whip. He did not need to touch the reins. Once on the rough road, between hedges twisting out to twig the mare by the bridle and poke our caps, we stopped at a whispered, 'Whoa,' for uncle to light his pipe and set the darkness on fire and show his long, red, drunken fox's face to me, with its bristling side-bushes and wet, sensitive nose. A white house with a light in one bedroom window shone in a field on a short hill beyond the road.

Uncle whispered, 'Easy, easy, girl,' to the mare, though she was standing calmly, and said to me over his shoulder in a suddenly loud voice, 'A hangman lived there.'

He stamped on the shaft, and we rattled on through a cutting wind. Uncle shivered, pulling down his cap to hide his ears; but the mare was like a clumsy statue trotting, and all the demons of my stories, if they trotted by her side or crowded together and grinned into her eyes, would not make her shake her head or hurry.

'I wish he'd have hung Mrs. Jesus,' uncle said.

Between hymns he cursed the mare in Welsh. The white house was left behind, the light and the hill were swallowed up.

'Nobody lives there now,' he said.

We drove into the farm-yard of Gorsehill, where the cobbles rang and the black, empty stables took up the ringing and hollowed it so that we drew up in a hollow circle of darkness and the mare was a hollow animal and nothing lived in the hollow house at the end of the yard but two sticks with faces scooped out of turnips.

'You run and see Annie,' said uncle. 'There'll be hot broth and potatoes.'

He led the hollow, shappy statue towards the stable;

clop, clop to the mice-house. I heard locks rattle as I ran to the farm-house door.

The front of the house was the single side of a black shell, and the arched door was the listening ear. I pushed the door open and walked into the passage out of the wind. I might have been walking into the hollow night and the wind, passing through a tall vertical shell on an inland sea-shore. Then a door at the end of the passage opened; I saw the plates on the shelves, the lighted lamp on the long, oil-clothed table, 'Prepare to Meet Thy God' knitted over the fire-place, the smiling china dogs, the brown-stained settle, the grandmother clock, and I ran into the kitchen and into Annie's arms.

There was a welcome, then. The clock struck twelve as she kissed me, and I stood among the shining and striking like a prince taking off his disguise. One minute I was small and cold, skulking dead-scared down a black passage in my stiff, best suit, with my hollow belly thumping and my heart like a time bomb, clutching my grammar school cap, unfamiliar to myself, a snub-nosed story-teller lost in his own adventures and longing to be home; the next I was a royal nephew in smart town clothes, embraced and welcomed, standing in the snug centre of my stories and listening to the clock announcing me. She hurried me to the seat in the side of the cavernous fireplace and took off my shoes. The bright lamps and the ceremonial gongs blazed and rang for me.

She made a mustard bath and strong tea, told me to put on a pair of my cousin Gwilym's socks and an old coat of uncle's that smelt of rabbit and tobacco. She fussed and clucked and nodded and told me, as she cut bread and butter, how Gwilym was still studying to be a minister, and how Aunt Rach Morgan, who was ninety years old, had fallen on her belly on a scythe.

Then Uncle Jim came in like the devil with a red face and a wet nose and trembling, hairy hands. His walk was thick. He stumbled against the dresser and shook the coronation plates, and a lean cat shot booted out from the settle corner. Uncle looked nearly twice as tall as Annie. He could have carried her about under his coat and brought her out suddenly, a little, brown-skinned, toothless, hunchbacked woman with a cracked sing-song voice.

'You shouldn't have kept him out so long,' she said, angry and timid.

He sat down in his special chair, which was the broken throne of a bankrupt bard, and lit his pipe and stretched his legs and puffed clouds at the ceiling.

'He might catch his death of cold,' she said.

She talked at the back of his head while he wrapped himself in clouds. The cat slunk back. I sat at the table with my supper finished, and found a little empty bottle and a white balloon in the pockets of my coat.

'Run off to bed, there's a dear,' Annie whispered.

'Can I go and look at the pigs?'

'In the morning, dear,' she said.

So I said good night to Uncle Jim, who turned and smiled at me and winked through the smoke, and I kissed Annie and lit my candle.

'Good night.'

'Good night.'

'Good night.'

I climbed the stairs; each had a different voice. The house smelt of rotten wood and damp and animals. I thought that I had been walking long, damp passages all my life, and climbing stairs in the dark, alone. I stopped outside Gwilym's door on the draughty landing.

'Good night.'

The candle flame jumped in my bedroom where a lamp was burning very low, and the curtains waved; the water in a glass on a round table by the bed stirred, I thought, as the door closed, and lapped against the sides. There was a stream below the window; I thought it lapped against the house all night until I slept.

'Can I go and see the pigs?' I asked Gwilym next morning. The hollow fear of the house was gone, and, running downstairs to my breakfast, I smelt the sweetness of wood and the fresh spring grass and the quiet untidy farm-yard, with its tumbledown dirty-white cow-house and empty stables open.

Gwilym was a tall young man aged nearly twenty, with a thin stick of a body and spade-shaped face. You could dig the garden with him. He had a deep voice that cracked in half when he was excited, and he sang songs to himself, treble and bass, with the same sad hymn tune, and wrote hymns in the barn. He told me stories about girls who died for love. 'And she put a rope round the tree but it was too short,' he said; 'she stuck a pen-knife in her bosoms but it was too blunt.' We were sitting together on the straw heaps that day in the half-dark of the shuttered stable. He twisted and leaned near to me, raising his big finger, and the straw creaked.

'She jumped in the cold river, she jumped,' he said, his mouth against my ear, 'arse over tip and Diu, she was dead.' He squeaked like a bat.

The pigsties were at the far end of the yard. We walked towards them, Gwilym dressed in minister's black, though it was a weekday morning, and me in a serge suit with a darned bottom, past three hens scrabbling the muddy cobbles and a collie with one eye, sleeping with it open. The ramshackle outhouses had tumbling, rotten roofs, jagged holes in their sides, broken shutters, and peeling whitewash; rusty screws ripped out from the dangling, crooked boards; the lean cat of the night before sat snugly between the splintered jaws of bottles, cleaning its face, on the tip of the rubbish pile that rose triangular and smelling sweet and strong to the level of the riddled cart-house roof. There was nowhere like that farm-yard in all the slapdash country, nowhere so poor and grand and dirty as that square of mud and rubbish and bad wood, and falling stone, where a bucketful of old and bedraggled hens scratched and laid small eggs. A duck quacked out of the trough in one deserted sty. Now a young man and a curly boy stood staring and sniffing over a wall at a sow, with its tits on the mud, giving suck.

'How many pigs are there?'

'Five. The bitch ate one,' said Gwilym.

We counted them as they squirmed and wriggled, rolled on their backs and bellies, edged and pinched and pushed and squealed about their mother. There were four. We counted again. Four pigs, four naked pink tails curling up as their mouths guzzled down and the sow grunted with pain and joy.

'She must have ate another,' I said, and picked up a scratching stick and prodded the grunting sow and rubbed her crusted bristles backward. 'Or a fox jumped over the wall,' I said.

'It wasn't the sow or the fox,' said Gwilym. 'It was father.'

I could see uncle, tall and sly and red, holding the

writing pig in his two hairy hands, sinking his teeth in its thigh, crunching its trotters up; I could see him leaning over the wall of the sty with the pig's legs sticking out of his mouth. 'Did Uncle Jim eat the pig?'

Now, at this minute, behind the rotting sheds, he was standing, knee-deep in feathers, chewing off the live heads of the poultry.

'He sold it to go on the drink,' said Gwilym in his deepest rebuking whisper, his eyes fixed on the sky. 'Last Christmas he took a sheep over his shoulder, and he was pissed for ten days.'

The sow rolled nearer the scratching stick, and the small pigs sucking at her, lost and squealing in the sudden darkness, struggled under her folds and pouches.

'Come and see my chapel,' said Gwilym. He forgot the lost pig at once and began to talk about the towns he had visited on a religious tour, Neath and Bridgend and Bristol and Newport, with their lakes and luxury gardens, their bright, coloured streets roaring with temptation. We walked away from the sty and the disappointed sow.

'I met actress after actress,' he said.

Gwilym's chapel was the last old barn before the field that led down to the river; it stood well above the farm-yard, on a mucky hill. There was one whole door with a heavy padlock, but you could get in easily through the holes on either side of it. He took out a ring of keys and shook them gently and tried each one in the lock. 'Very posh,' he said; 'I bought them from the junk-shop in Carmarthen.' We climbed into the chapel through a hole.

A dusty wagon with the name painted out and a white-wash cross on its side stood in the middle. 'My pulpit cart,' he said, and walked solemnly into it up the broken shaft. 'You sit on the hay; mind the mice,' he said. Then he brought out his deepest voice again, and cried to the heavens and the bat-lined rafters and the hanging webs, 'Bless us this holy day, O Lord, bless me and Dylan and this Thy little chapel for ever and ever, Amen. I've done a lot of improvements to this place.'

I sat on the hay and stared at Gwilym preaching, and heard his voice rise and crack and sink to a whisper and break into singing and Welsh and ring triumphantly and be wild and meek. The sun through a hole, shone on his praying shoulders, and he said, 'O God, Thou art everywhere all the time, in the dew of the morning, in the frost of the evening, in the field and the town, in the preacher and sinner, in the sparrow and the big buzzard. Thou canst see everything, right down deep in our hearts; Thou canst see us when the sun is gone; Thou canst see us when there aren't any stars, in the gravy blackness, in the deep, deep, deep, deep pit; Thou canst see and spy and watch us all the time, in the little black corners, in the big cowboys' prairies, under the blankets when we're snoring fast, in the terrible shadows; pitch black, pitch black; Thou canst see everything we do, in the night and day, in the day and night, everything, everything; Thou canst see all the time. O God, mun, you're like a bloody cat.'

He let his clasped hands fall. The chapel in the barn was still, and shafted with sunlight. There was nobody to cry Hallelujah or God-bless; I was too small and enamoured in the silence. The one duck quacked outside.

'Now I take a collection,' Gwilym said.

He stepped down from the cart and groped about in the hay beneath it and held out a battered tin to me.

'I haven't got a proper box,' he said.

I put two pennies in the tin.

'It's time for dinner,' he said, and we went back to the house without a word.

Annie said, when we had finished dinner, 'Put on your nice suit for this afternoon. The one with stripes.'

It was to be a special afternoon, for my best friend, Jack Williams, from Swansea, was coming down with his rich mother in a motor car, and Jack was to spend a fortnight's holiday with me.

'Where's Uncle Jim?'

'He's gone to market,' said Annie.

Gwilym made a small pig's noise. We knew where uncle was; he was sitting in a public house with a heifer over his shoulder and two pigs nosing out of his pockets, and his lips wet with bull's blood.

'Is Mrs. Williams very rich?' asked Gwilym.

I told him she had three motor cars and two houses, which was a lie. 'She's the richest woman in Wales; and once she was a mayoress,' I said. 'Are we going to have tea in the best room?'

Annie nodded. 'And a large tin of peaches,' she said.

'That old tin's been in the cupboard since Christmas,' said Gwilym, 'mother's been keeping it for a day like this.'

'They're lovely peaches,' Annie said. She went upstairs to dress like Sunday.

The best room smelt of moth balls and fur and damp and dead plants and stale, sour air. Two glass cases on wooden coffin-boxes lined the window wall. You looked at the weed-grown vegetable garden through a stuffed fox's legs, over a partridge's head, along the red-paint-stained breast of a stiff wild duck. A case of china and pewter, trinkets, teeth, family brooches, stood beyond the bandy table; there was a large oil lamp on the patchwork table-cloth, a Bible, with a clasp, a tall vase with a draped woman about to bathe on it, and a framed photograph of Annie, Uncle Jim, and Gwilym smiling in front of a fern-pot. On the mantelpiece were two clocks, some dogs, brass candlesticks, a shepherdess, a man in a kilt, and a tinted photograph of Annie, with high hair and her breasts coming out. There were chairs around the table and in each corner, straight, curved, stained, padded, all with lace cloths hanging over their backs. A patched white sheet shrouded the harmonium. The fireplace was full of brass tongs, shovels, and pokers. The best room was rarely used. Annie dusted and brushed and polished there once a week, but the carpet still sent up a grey cloud when you trod on it, and dust lay evenly on the seats of the chairs, and balls of cotton and dirt and black stuffing and long black horse hairs were wedged in the cracks of the sofa. I blew on the glass to see the pictures. Gwilym and castles and cattle.

'Change your suit now,' said Gwilym.

I wanted to wear my old suit, to look like a proper farm boy and have manure in my shoes and hear it squelch as I walked, to see a cow have calves and a bull on top of a cow, to run down in the dingle and wet my stockings, to go out and shout, 'Come on, you b——,' and pelt the hens and talk in a proper voice. But I went upstairs to put my striped suit on.

From my bedroom I heard the noise of a motor car drawing up in the yard. It was Jack Williams and his mother.

Gwilym shouted, 'They're here, in a Daimler!' from the foot of the stairs, and I ran down to meet them with my tie undone and my hair uncombed.

Annie was saying at the door, 'Good afternoon, Mrs. Williams, good afternoon. Come right in, it's a lovely day, Mrs. Williams. Did you have a nice journey then? This way, Mrs. Williams, mind the step.'

Annie wore a black, shining dress that smelt of moth balls, like the chair covers in the best room; she had forgotten to change her gym-shoes, which were caked with mud and all holes. She fussed on before Mrs. Williams down the stone passage, darting her head round, clucking, fidgeting, excusing the small house, anxiously tidying her hair with one rough, stubby hand.

Mrs. Williams was tall and stout, with a jutting bosom and thick legs, her ankles swollen over her pointed shoes; she was fitted out like a mayoress or a ship, and she swayed after Annie into the best room.

She said, 'Please don't put yourself out for me, Mrs. Jones, there's a dear.' She dusted the seat of a chair with a lace handkerchief from her bag before sitting down.

'I can't stop, you know,' she said.

'Oh, you must stay for a cup of tea,' said Annie, shifting and scraping the chairs away from the table so that nobody could move and Mrs. Williams was hemmed in fast with her bosom and her rings and her bag, opening the china cupboard, upsetting the Bible on the floor, picking it up, dusting it hurriedly with her sleeve.

'And peaches,' Gwilym said. He was standing in the passage with his hat on.

Annie said, 'Take your hat off, Gwilym, make Mrs. Williams comfortable,' and she put the lamp on the shrouded harmonium and spread out a white table-cloth that had a tea stain in the centre, and brought out the china and laid knives and cups for five.

'Don't bother about me, there's a dear,' said Mrs. Williams. 'There's a lovely fox!' She flashed a finger of rings at the glass case.

'It's real blood,' I told Jack, and we climbed over the sofa to the table.

'No, it isn't,' he said, 'it's red ink.'

'Oh, your shoes!' said Annie.

'Don't tread on the sofa, Jack, there's a dear.'

'If it isn't ink it's paint then.'

Gwilym said, 'Shall I get you a bit of cake, Mrs. Williams?'

Annie rattled the tea-cups. 'There isn't a single bit of cake in the house,' she said; 'we forgot to order it from the shop; not a single bit. Oh, Mrs. Williams!'

Mrs. Williams said, 'Just a cup of tea thanks.' She was still sweating because she had walked all the way from the car. It spoiled her powder. She sparkled her rings and dabbed at her face.

'Three lumps,' she said. 'And I'm sure Jack will be very happy here.'

'Happy as sandboys.' Gwilym sat down.

'Now you must have some peaches, Mrs. Williams, they're lovely.'

'They should be, they've been here long enough,' said Gwilym.

Annie rattled the tea-cups at him again.

'No peaches, thanks,' Mrs. Williams said.

'Oh, you must, Mrs. Williams, just one. With cream.'

'No, no, Mrs. Jones, thanks the same,' she said. 'I don't mind pears or chunks, but I can't bear peaches.'

Jack and I had stopped talking. Annie stared down at

her gym-shoes. One of the clocks on the mantelpiece coughed, and struck. Mrs. Williams struggled from her chair.

'There, time flies!' she said.

She pushed her way past the furniture, jostled against the sideboard, rattled the trinkets and brooches, and kissed Jack on the forehead.

'You've got scent on,' he said.

She patted my head.

'Now behave yourselves.'

To Annie, she said in a whisper, 'And remember, Mrs. Jones, just good plain food. No spoiling his appetite.'

Annie followed her out of the room. She moved slowly now. 'I'll do my very best, Mrs. Williams.'

We heard her say, 'Good-bye then, Mrs. Williams,' and go down the steps of the kitchen and close the door. The motor car roared in the yard, then the noise grew softer and died.

Down the thick dingle Jack and I ran shouting, scalping the brambles with our thin stick-hatchets, dancing, hallooing. We skidded to a stop and prowled on the bushy banks of the stream. Up above, sat one-eyed, dead-eyed, sinister, slim, ten-notched Gwilym, loading his guns in Gallows Farm. We crawled and rat-tatted through the bushes, hid, at a whistled signal, in the deep grass, and crouched there, waiting for the crack of a twig or the secret breaking of boughs.

On my haunches, eager and alone, casting an ebony shadow, with the Gorsehill jungle swarming, the violent, impossible birds and fishes leaping, hidden under four-stemmed flowers the height of horses, in the early evening in a dingle near Carmarthen, my friend Jack Williams

invisibly near me, I felt all my young body like an excited animal surrounding me, the torn knees bent, the bumping heart, the long heat and depth between the legs, the sweat prickling in the hands, the tunnels down to the eardrums, the little balls of dirt between the toes, the eyes in the sockets, the tucked-up voice, the blood racing, the memory around and within flying, jumping, swimming, and waiting to pounce. There, playing Indians in the evening, I was aware of me myself in the exact middle of a living story, and my body was my adventure and my name. I sprang with excitement and scrambled up through the scratching brambles again.

Jack cried, 'I see you! I see you!' He scampered after me. 'Bang! Bang! You're dead!'

But I was young and loud and alive, though I lay down obediently.

'Now you try and kill me,' said Jack. 'Count a hundred.'

I closed one eye, saw him rush and stamp towards the upper field, then tiptoe back and begin to climb a tree, and I counted fifty and ran to the foot of the tree and killed him as he climbed. 'You fall down,' I said.

He refused to fall, so I climbed too, and we clung to the top branches and stared down at the lavatory in the corner of the field. Gwilym was sitting on the seat with his trousers down. He looked small and black. He was reading a book and moving his hands.

'We can see you!' we shouted.

He snatched his trousers up and put the book in his pocket.

'We can see you, Gwilym!'

He came out into the field. 'Where are you, then?'

We waved our caps at him.

'In the sky!' Jack shóuted.

'Flying!' I shouted.

We stretched our arms out like wings.

'Fly down here.'

We swung and laughed on the branches.

'There's birds!' cried Gwilym.

Our jackets were torn and our stockings were wet and our shoes were sticky; we had green moss and brown bark on our hands and faces when we went in for supper and a scolding. Annie was quiet that night, though she called me a ragamuffin and said she didn't know what Mrs. Williams would think and told Gwilym he should know better. We made faces at Gwilym and put salt in his tea, but after supper he said, 'You can come to the chapel if you like. Just before bed.'

He lit a candle on the top of the pulpit cart. It was a small light in the big barn. The bats were gone. Shadows still clung upside down along the roof. Gwilym was no longer my cousin in a Sunday suit, but a tall stranger shaped like a spade in a cloak, and his voice grew too deep. The straw heaps were lively. I thought of the sermon on the cart: we were watched, Jack's heart was watched. Gwilym's tongue was marked down, my whisper, 'Look at the little eyes,' was remembered always.

'Now I take confessions,' said Gwilym from the cart.

Jack and I stood bareheaded in the circle of the candle, and I could feel the trembling of Jack's body.

'You first.' Gwilym's finger, as bright as though he had held it in the candle flame until it burned, pointed me out, and I took a step towards the pulpit cart, raising my head.

'Now you confess,' said Gwilym.

'What have I got to confess?'

'The worst thing you've done.'

I let Edgar Reynolds be whipped because I had taken his homework; I stole from my mother's bag; I stole from Gwyneth's bag; I stole twelve books in three visits from the library, and threw them away in the park; I drank a cup of my water to see what it tasted like; I beat a dog with a stick so that it would roll over and lick my hand afterwards; I looked with Dan Jones through the keyhole while his maid had a bath; I cut my knee with a penknife, and put the blood on my handkerchief and said it had come out of my ears so that I could pretend I was ill and frighten my mother; I pulled my trousers down and showed Jack Williams; I saw Billy Jones beat a pigeon to death with a fire-shovel, and laughed and got sick; Cedric Williams and I broke into Mrs. Samuels' house and poured ink over the bedclothes.

I said, 'I haven't done anything bad.'

'Go on, confess,' said Gwilym. He was frowning down at me.

'I can't! I can't!' I said. 'I haven't done anything bad.'

'Go on, confess!'

'I won't! I won't!'

Jack began to cry. 'I want to go home,' he said.

Gwilym opened the chapel door and we followed him into the yard, down past the black, humped sheds, towards the house, and Jack sobbed all the way.

In bed together, Jack and I confessed our sins.

'I steal from my mother's bag, too; there are pounds and pounds.'

'How much do you steal?'

'Threepence.'

'I killed a man once.'

'No you didn't then.'

'Honest to Christ, I shot him through the heart.'

'What was his name?'

'Williams.'

'Did he bleed?'

I thought the stream was lapping against the house.

'Like a bloody pig,' I said.

Jack's tears had dried. 'I don't like Gwilym, he's barmy.'

'No he isn't. I found a lot of poems in his bedroom once. They were all written to girls. And he showed them to me afterwards, and he'd changed all the girls' names to God.'

'He's religious.'

'No he isn't, he goes with actresses. He knows Corinne Griffith.'

Our door was open. I liked the door locked at night, because I would rather have a ghost in the bedroom than think of one coming in; but Jack liked it open, and we tossed and he won. We heard the front door rattle and footsteps in the kitchen passage.

'That's Uncle Jim.'

'What's he like?'

'He's like a fox, he eats pigs and chickens.'

The ceiling was thin and we heard every sound, the creaking of the bard's chair, the clatter of plates, Annie's voice saying, 'Midnight!'

'He's drunk,' I said. We lay quite still, hoping to hear a quarrel.

'Perhaps he'll throw plates,' I said.

But Annie scolded him softly, 'There's a fine state, Jim.'
He murmured to her.

'There's one pig gone,' she said. 'Oh, why do you have
to do it, Jim? There's nothing left now. We'll never be
able to carry on.'

'Money! Money! Money!' he said. I knew he would be
lighting his pipe.

Then Annie's voice grew so soft we could not hear the
words, and uncle said, 'Did she pay you the thirty shill-
ings?'

'They're talking about your mother,' I told Jack.

For a long time Annie spoke in a low voice, and we
waited for words. 'Mrs. Williams,' she said, and 'motor
car,' and 'Jack,' and 'peaches.' I thought she was crying
for her voice broke on the last word.

Uncle Jim's chair creaked again, he might have struck
his fist on the table, and we heard him shout, 'I'll give her
peaches! Peaches, peaches! Who does she think she is?
Aren't peaches good enough for her? To hell with her
bloody motor car and her bloody son! Making us small!'

'Don't, don't Jim!' Annie said, 'You'll wake the boys.'

'I'll wake them and whip the hell out of them, too!'

'Please, please, Jim!'

'You send the boy away,' he said, 'or I'll do it myself.
Back to his three bloody houses.'

Jack pulled the bedclothes over his head and sobbed
into the pillow, 'I don't want to hear, I don't want to
hear. I'll write to my mother. She'll take me away.'

I climbed out to close the door. Jack would not talk to
me again, and I fell asleep to the noise of the voices
below, which soon grew gentle.

Uncle Jim was not at breakfast. When we came down,

Jack's shoes were cleaned for him and his jacket was darned and pressed. Annie gave two boiled eggs to Jack and one to me. She forgave me when I drank tea from the saucer.

After breakfast, Jack walked to the post office. I took the one-eyed collie to chase rabbits in the upper fields, but it barked at ducks and brought me a tramp's shoe from a hedge, and lay down with its tail wagging in a rabbit hole. I threw stones at the deserted duck pond, and the collie ambled back with sticks.

Jack went skulking into the damp dingle, his hands in his pockets, his cap over one eye. I left the collie sniffing at a molehill, and climbed to the tree-top in the corner of the lavatory field. Below me, Jack was playing Indians all alone, scalping through the bushes, surprising himself round a tree, hiding from himself in the grass. I called to him once, but he pretended not to hear. He played alone, silently and savagely. I saw him standing with his hands in his pockets, swaying like a Kelly, on the mudbank by the stream at the foot of the dingle. My bough lurched, the heads of the dingle bushes spun up towards me like green tops, 'I'm falling!' I cried, my trousers saved me, I swung and grasped, this was one minute of wild adventure, but Jack did not look up and the minute was lost. I climbed, without dignity, to the ground.

Early in the afternoon, after a silent meal, when Gwilym was reading the scriptures or writing hymns to girls or sleeping in his chapel, Annie was baking bread, and I was cutting a wooden whistle in the loft over the stable, the motor car drove up in the yard again.

Out of the house Jack, in his best suit, ran to meet his mother, and I heard him say as she stepped, raising her short skirts, on to the cobbles, 'And he called you a bloody cow, and he said he'd whip the hell out of me, and Gwilym took me to the barn in the dark and let the mice run over me, and Dylan's a thief, and that old woman's spoilt my jacket.'

Mrs. Williams sent the chauffeur for Jack's luggage. Annie came to the door, trying to smile and curtsy, tidying her hair, wiping her hands on her pinafore.

Mrs. Williams said, 'Good afternoon,' and sat with Jack in the back of the car and stared at the ruin of Gorsehill.

The chauffeur came back. The car drove off, scattering the hens. I ran out of the stable to wave to Jack. He sat still and stiff by his mother's side. I waved my handkerchief.

Who Do You Wish Was with Us?

Birds in the Crescent trees were singing; boys on bicycles were ringing their bells and pedalling down the slight slope to make the whirrers in their wheels startle the women gabbing on the sunny doorsteps; small girls on the pavement, wheeling young brothers and sisters in prams, were dressed in their summer best and with coloured ribbons; on the circular swing in the public playground, children from the snot school spun themselves happy and sick, crying, 'Swing us!' and 'Swing us!' and 'Ooh! I'm falling!'; the morning was as varied and bright as though it were an international or a jubilee when Raymond Price and I, flannelled and hatless, with sticks and haversacks, set out together to walk to the Worm's Head. Striding along, in step, through the square of the residential Uplands, we brushed by young men in knife-creased whites and showing-off blazers, and hockey-legged girls with towels round their necks and celluloid sun-glasses, and struck a letterbox with our sticks, and bullied our way through a crowd of day-trippers who waited at the stop of the Gower-bound buses, and stepped over luncheon baskets, not caring if we trod in them.

'Why can't those bus lizards walk?' Ray said.

'They were born too tired,' I said.

We went on up Sketty Road at a great speed, our haversacks jumping on our backs. We rapped on every gate to give a terrific walker's benediction to the people in the choking houses. Like a breath of fresh air we passed a man in office pin-stripes standing, with a dog-lead in his hand, whistling at a corner. Tossing the sounds and smells of the town from us with the swing of our shoulders and loose-limbed strides, half-way up the road we heard women on an outing call, 'Mutt and Jeff!' for Ray was tall and thin and I was short. Streamers flew out of the charabanc. Ray, sucking hard at his bulldog pipe, walked too fast to wave and did not even smile. I wondered whom I had missed among the waving women bowling over the rise. My love to come, with a paper cap on, might have sat at the back of the outing, next to the barrel; but, once away from the familiar roads and swinging towards the coast, I forgot her face and voice, that had been made at night, and breathed the country air in.

'There's a different air here. You breathe. It's like the country,' Ray said, 'and a bit of the sea mixed. Draw it down; it'll blow off the nicotine.'

He spat in his hand. 'Still town-grey,' he said.

He put back the spit in his mouth and we walked on with our heads high.

By this time we were three miles from the town. The semi-detached houses, with a tin-roofed garage each and a kennel in the back plot and a mowed lawn, with sometimes a hanging coconut on a pole, or a bird-bath, or a bush like a peacock, grew fewer when we reached the outskirts of the common.

Ray stopped and sighed and said, 'Wait half a sec, I

74

want to fill the old pipe.' He held a match to it as though we were in a storm.

Hot-faced and wet-browed, we grinned at each other. Already the day had brought us close as truants; we were running away, or walking with pride and mischief, arrogantly from the streets that owned us into the unpredictable country. I thought it was against our fate to stride in the sun without the shop-windows dazzling or the music of mowers rising above the birds. A bird's dropping fell on a fence. It was one in the eye for the town. A sheep cried, 'Baa!' out of sight, and that would show the Uplands. I did not know what it would show. 'A couple of wanderers in wild Wales,' Ray said, winking, and a lorry carrying cement drove past us towards the golf links. He slapped my haversack and straightened his shoulders. 'Come on, let's be going.' We walked uphill faster than before.

A party of cyclists had pulled up on the roadside and were drinking dandelion and burdock from paper cups. I saw the empty bottles in a bush. All the boys wore singlets and shorts, and the girls wore open cricket shirts and boys' long grey trousers, with safety-pins for clips at the bottoms.

'There's room for one behind, sonny boy,' a girl on a tandem said to me.

'It won't be a stylish marriage,' Ray said.

'That was quick,' I told Ray as we walked away from them and the boys began to sing.

'God, I like this!' said Ray. On the first rise of the dusty road through the spreading heathered common, he shaded his eyes and looked all round him, smoking like a chimney and pointing with his Irish stick at the distant clumps of trees and sights of the sea between them. 'Down there is Oxwich, but you can't see it. That's a farm. See the roof? No, there, follow my finger. This is the life,' he said.

Side by side, thrashing the low banks, we marched down the very middle of the road, and Ray saw a rabbit running. 'You wouldn't think this was near town. It's wild.'

We pointed out the birds whose names we knew, and the rest of the names we made up. I saw gulls and crows, though the crows may have been rooks, and Ray said that thrushes and swallows and skylarks flew above us as we hurried and hummed.

He stopped to pull some blades of grass. 'They should be straws,' he said, and put them in his mouth next to his pipe. 'God, the sky's blue! Think of me, in the G.W.R. when all this is about. Rabbits and fields and farms. You wouldn't think I'd suffered to look at me now. I could do anything, I could drive cows, I could plough a field.'

His father and sister and brother were dead, and his mother sat all day in a wheel-chair, crippled with arthritis. He was ten years older than I was. He had a lined and bony face and a tight, crooked mouth. His upper lip had vanished.

Alone on the long road, the common in the heat mist wasting for miles on either side, we walked on under the afternoon sun, growing thirsty and drowsy but never slowing our pace. Soon the cycling party rode by, three boys and three girls and the one girl on the tandem, all laughing and ringing.

'How's Shank's pony?'

'We'll see you on the way back.'

'You'll be walking still.'

'Like a crutch?' they shouted.

Then they were gone. The dust settled again. Their bells rang faintly through the wood around the road before us. The wild common, six miles and a bit from the town, lay back without a figure on it, and, under the trees, smoking hard to keep the gnats away, we leant against a trunk and talked like men, on the edge of an untrodden place, who have not seen another man for years.

'Do you remember Curly Parry?'

I had seen him only two days ago in the snooker-room, but his dimpled face was fading, even as I thought of him, into the colours of our walk, the ash-white of the road, the common heathers, the green and blue of fields and fragmentary sea, and the memory of his silly voice was lost in the sounds of birds and unreasonably moving leaves in the lack of wind.

'I wonder what he's doing now? He should get out more in the open air, he's a proper town boy. Look at us here.' Ray waved his pipe at the trees and leafy sky. 'I wouldn't change this for High Street.'

I looked at us there; a boy and a young man, with faces, under the strange sunburn, pale from the cramped town, out of breath and hot-footed, pausing in the early afternoon on a road through a popular wood, and I could see the unaccustomed happiness in Ray's eyes and the impossible friendliness in mine, and Ray protested against his history each time he wondered or pointed in the country scene and I had more love in me than I could ever want or use.

'Yes, look at us here,' I said, 'dawdling about. Worm's

Head is twelve miles off. Don't you want to hear a tramcar, Ray? That's a wood pigeon. See! The boys are out on the streets with the sports special now. Paper! Paper! I bet you Curl's potting the red. Come on! Come on!'

'Eyes right!' said Ray, 'I's b——d! Remember that story?'

Up the road and out of the wood, and a double-decker roared behind us.

'The Rhossilli bus is coming,' I said.

We both held up our sticks to stop it.

'Why did you stop the bus?' Ray said, when we were sitting upstairs. 'This was a walking holiday.'

'You stopped it as well.'

We sat in the front like two more drivers.

'Can't you mind the ruts?' I said.

'You're wobbling,' said Ray.

We opened our haversacks and shared the sandwiches and hard-boiled eggs and meat paste and drank from the thermos in turns.

'When we get home don't say we took a bus,' I said. 'Pretend we walked all day. There goes Oxwich! It doesn't seem far, does it? We'd have had beards by now.'

The bus passed the cyclists crawling up a hill. 'Like a tow along?' I shouted, but they couldn't hear. The girl on the tandem was a long way behind the others.

We sat with our lunch on our laps, forgetting to steer, letting the driver in his box beneath drive where and how he liked on the switch-back road, and saw grey chapels and weather-worn angels; at the feet of the hills farthest from the sea, pretty, pink cottages—horrible, I thought, to live in, for grass and trees would imprison me more

78

securely than any jungle of packed and swarming streets and chimney-roosting roofs—and petrol pumps and hay-ricks and a man on a cart-horse standing stock still in a ditch, surrounded by flies.

'This is the way to see the country.'

The bus, on a narrow hill, sent two haversacked walkers bounding to the shelter of the hedge, where they stretched out their arms and drew their bellies in.

'That might have been you and me.'

We looked back happily at the men against the hedge. They climbed on to the road, slow as snails continued walking, and grew smaller.

At the entrance to Rhossilli we pushed the conductor's bell and stopped the bus, and walked, with springing steps, the few hundred yards to the village.

'We've done it in pretty good time,' said Ray.

'I think it's a record,' I said.

Laughing on the cliff above the very long golden beach, we pointed out to each other, as though the other were blind, the great rock of the Worm's Head. The sea was out. We crossed over on slipping stones and stood, at last, triumphantly on the windy top. There was monstrous, thick grass there that made us spring-heeled, and we laughed and bounced on it, scaring the sheep who ran up and down the battered sides like goats. Even on this calmest day a wind blew along the Worm. At the end of the humped and serpentine body, more gulls than I had ever seen before cried over their new dead and the droppings of ages. On the point, the sound of my quiet voice was scooped and magnified into a hollow shout, as though the wind around me had made a shell or cave, with blue, intangible roof and sides, as tall and wide as all the arched sky, and the flapping gulls were made thunderous. Standing there, legs apart, one hand on my hip, shading my eyes like Raleigh in some picture, I thought myself alone in the epileptic moment near bad sleep, when the legs grow long and sprout into the night and the heart hammers to wake the neighbours and breath is a hurricane through the elastic room. Instead of becoming small on the great rock poised between sky and sea, I felt myself the size of a breathing building, and only Ray in the world could match my lovely bellow as I said, 'Why don't we live here always? Always and always. Build a bloody house and live like bloody kings!' The word bellowed among the squawking birds, they carried it off to the headland in the drums of their wings; like a tower, Ray pranced on the unsteady edge of a separate rock and beat about with his stick, which could turn into snakes or flames; and we sank to the ground, the rubbery, gull-limed grass, the sheep-pilled stones, the pieces of bones and feathers, and crouched at the extreme point of the Peninsula. We were still for so long that the dirty-grey gulls calmed down, and some settled near us.

Then we finished our food.

'This isn't like any other place,' I said. I was almost my own size again, five feet five and eight stone, and my voice didn't sweep any longer up to the amplifying sky. 'It could be in the middle of the sea. You could think the Worm was moving, couldn't you? Guide it to Ireland, Ray. We'll see W. B. Yeats and you can kiss the Blarney. We'll have a fight in Belfast.'

Ray looked out of place on the end of the rock. He would not make himself easy and loll in the sun and roll on to his side to stare down a precipice into the sea, but tried to sit upright as though he were in a hard chair and had nothing to do with his hands. He fiddled with his tame stick and waited for the day to be orderly, for the Head to grow paths and for railings to shoot up on the scarred edges.

'It's too wild for a townee,' I said.

'Townee yourself! Who stopped the bus?'

'Aren't you glad we stopped it? We'd still be walking, like Felix. You're just pretending you don't like it here. You were dancing on the edge.'

'Only a couple of hops.'

'I know what it is, you don't like the furniture. There's not enough sofas and chairs,' I said.

'You think you're a country boy; you don't know a cow from a horse.'

We began to quarrel, and soon Ray felt at home again and forgot the monotonous out-of-doors. If snow had fallen suddenly he would not have noticed. He drew down into himself, and the rock, to him, became dark as a house with the blinds drawn. The sky-high shapes that had danced and bellowed at birds crept down to hide, two small town mutterers in a hollow.

I knew what was going to happen by the way Ray lowered his head and brought his shoulders up so that he looked like a man with no neck, and by the way he sucked his breath in between his teeth. He stared at his dusty white shoes and I knew what shapes his imagination made of them; they were the feet of a man dead in bed, and he was going to talk about his brother. Sometimes, leaning against a fence when we watched football, I caught him staring at his own thin hand; he was thinning it more and more, removing the flesh, seeing

Harry's hand in front of him, with the bones appearing through the sensitive skin. If he lost the world around him for a moment, if I left him alone, if he cast his eyes down, if his hand lost its grip on the hard, real fence or the hot bowl of his pipe, he would be back in ghastly bedrooms, carrying cloths and basins and listening for handbells.

'I've never seen such a lot of gulls,' I said. 'Have you ever seen such a lot? Such a lot of gulls. You try and count them. Two of them are fighting up there; look, pecking at each other like hens in the air. What'll you bet the big one wins? Old dirty beak! I wouldn't like to have had his dinner, a bit of sheep and dead gull.' I swore at myself for saying the word 'dead'. 'Wasn't it gay in town this morning?' I said.

Ray stared at his hand. Nothing could stop him now. 'Wasn't it gay in town this morning? Everybody laughing and smiling in their summer outfits. The kids were play-ing and everybody was happy; they almost had the band out. I used to hold my father down on the bed when he had fits. I had to change the sheets twice a day for my brother, there was blood on everything. I watched him getting thinner and thinner; in the end you could lift him up with one hand. And his wife wouldn't go to see him because he coughed in her face. Mother couldn't move, and I had to cook as well, cook and nurse and change the sheets and hold father down when he got mad. It's embittered my outlook,' he said.

'But you loved the walk, you enjoyed yourself on the common. It's a wonderful day, Ray. I'm sorry about your brother. Let's explore. Let's climb down to the sea. Perhaps there's a cave with prehistoric drawings, and we can write an article and make a fortune. Let's climb down.'

'My brother used to ring a bell for me; he could only whisper. He used to say, "Ray, look at my legs. Are they thinner today?" '

'The sun is going down. Let's climb.'

'Father thought I was trying to murder him when I held him on the bed. I was holding him down when he died, and he rattled. Mother was in the kitchen in her chair, but she knew he was dead and she started screaming for my sister. Brenda was in a sanatorium in Craigynos. Harry rang the bell in his bedroom when mother started, but I couldn't go to him, and father was dead in the bed.'

'I'm going to climb to the sea,' I said. 'Are you coming?'

He got up out of the hollow into the open world again and followed me slowly over the point and down the steep side; the gulls rose in a storm. I clung to dry, spiked bushes but the roots came out; a foothold crumbled, a crevice for the fingers broke as I groped in it; I scrambled on to a black, flat-backed rock whose head, like a little Worm's, curved out of the sea a few perilous steps away from me, and, drenched by flying water, I gazed up to see Ray and a shower of stones falling. He landed at my side.

'I thought I was done for,' he said, when he had stopped shaking. 'I could see all my past life in a flash.'

'All of it?'

'Well, nearly. I saw my brother's face clear as yours.'

We watched the sun set.

'Like an orange.'

'Like a tomato.'

'Like a goldfish bowl.'

We went one better than the other, describing the sun. The sea beat on our rock, soaked our trouser-legs, stung our cheeks. I took off my shoes and held Ray's hand and slid down the rock on my belly to trail my feet in the sea. Then Ray slid down, and I held him fast while he kicked up water.

'Come back now,' I said, pulling his hand.

'No, no,' he said, 'this is delicious. Let me keep my feet in a bit more. It's warm as the baths.' He kicked and grunted and slapped the rock in a frenzy with his other hand, pretending to drown. 'Don't save me!' he cried. 'I'm drowning! I'm drowning!'

I pulled him back, and in his struggles he brushed a shoe off the rock. We fished it out. It was full of water.

'Never mind, it was worth it. I haven't paddled since I was six. I can't tell you how much I enjoyed it.'

He had forgotten about his father and his brother, but I knew that once his joy in the wild, warm water was over he would return to the painful house and see his brother growing thinner. I had heard Harry die so many times, and the mad father was as familiar to me as Ray himself. I knew every cough and cry, every clawing at the air.

'I'm going to paddle once a day from now on,' Ray said. 'I'm going to go down to the sands every evening and have a good paddle. I'm going to splash about and get wet up to my knees. I don't care who laughs.'

He sat still for a minute, thinking gravely of this. 'When I wake up in the mornings there's nothing to look forward to, except on Saturdays,' he said then, 'or when I come up to your house for Lexicon. I may as well be dead. But now I'll be able to wake up and think, this evening I'm going to splash about in the sea. I'm going to do it again now.' He rolled up his wet trousers and slid down the rock. 'Don't let go.'

As he kicked his legs in the sea, I said, 'This is a rock at the world's end. We're all alone. It all belongs to us, Ray. We can have anybody we like here and keep everybody else away. Who do you wish was with us?'

He was too busy to answer, splashing and snorting, blowing as though his head were under, making circular commotions in the water or lazily skimming the surface with his toes.

'Who would you like to be here on the rock with us?'

He was stretched out like a dead man, his feet motionless in the sea, his mouth on the rim of a rock pool, his hand clutched round my foot.

'I wish George Gray was with us,' I said. 'He's the man from London who's come to live in Norfolk Street. You don't know him. He's the most curious man I ever met, queerer than Oscar Thomas, and I thought nobody could ever be queerer than that. George Gray wears glasses, but there's no glass in them, only the frames. You wouldn't know until you came near him. He does all sorts of things. He's a cat's doctor and he goes to somewhere in Sketty every morning to help a woman put her clothes on. She's an old widow, he said, and she can't dress by herself. I don't know how he came to know her. He's only been in town for a month. He's a B.A., too. The things he's got in his pockets! Pincers, and scissors for cats, and lots of diaries. He read me some of the diaries, about the jobs he did in London. He used to go to bed with a police-woman and she used to pay him. She used to go to bed in her uniform. I've never met such a queer man. I wish he was here now. Who do you wish was with us, Ray?'

Ray began to move his feet again, kicking them out straight behind him and bringing them down hard on the water, and then stirring the water about.

'I wish Gwilym was here, too,' I said. 'I've told you about him. He could give a sermon to the sea. This is the very place, there isn't anywhere as lonely as this.' Oh, the beloved sunset! Oh, the terrible sea! Pity the sailors, pity the sinners, pity Raymond Price and me! Oh, the evening is coming like a cloud! Amen. Amen. 'Who do you wish, Ray?'

'I wish my brother was with us,' Ray said. He climbed on to the flat of the rock and dried his feet. 'I wish Harry was here. I wish he was here now, at this moment, on this rock.'

The sun was nearly right down, halved by the shadowed sea. Cold came up, spraying out of the sea, and I could make a body for it, icy antlers, a dripping tail, a rippling face with fishes passing across it. A wind, cornering the Head, chilled through our summer shirts, and the sea began to cover our rock quickly, our rock already covered with friends, with living and dead, racing against the darkness. We did not speak as we climbed. I thought, if we open our mouths we'll both say, 'Too late, it's too late.' We ran over the spring-board grass and the scraping rock needles, down the hollow in which Ray had talked about blood, up rustling humps, and along the ragged flat. We stood on the beginning of the Head and looked down, though both of us could have said, without looking, 'The sea is in.'

The sea was in. The slipping stepping-stones were gone. On the mainland, in the dusk, some little figures beckoned to us. Seven clear figures, jumping and calling. I thought they were the cyclists.

The Fight

I was standing at the end of the lower playground and annoying Mr. Samuels, who lived in the house just below the high railings. Mr. Samuels complained once a week that boys from the school threw apples and stones and balls through his bedroom window. He sat in a deck chair in a small square of trim garden and tried to read the newspaper. I was only a few yards from him. I was staring him out. He pretended not to notice me, but I knew he knew I was standing there rudely and quietly. Every now and then he peeped at me from behind his newspaper, saw me still and serious and alone, with my eyes on his. As soon as he lost his temper I was going to go home. Already I was late for dinner. I had almost beaten him, the newspaper was trembling, he was breathing heavily, when a strange boy, whom I had not heard approach, pushed me down the bank.

I threw a stone at his face. He took off his spectacles, put them in his coat pocket, took off his coat, hung it neatly on the railings, and attacked. Turning round as we wrestled on the top of the bank, I saw that Mr. Samuels had folded his newspaper on the deck chair and was standing up to watch us. It was a mistake to turn round. The strange boy rabbit-punched me twice. Mr. Samuels hopped with excitement as I fell against the railings. I was

down in the dust, hot and scratched and biting, then up and dancing, and I butted the boy in the belly and we tumbled in a heap. I saw through a closing eye that his nose was bleeding. I hit his nose. He tore at my collar and spun me round by the hair.

'Come on! Come on!' I heard Mr. Samuels cry.

We both turned towards him. He was shaking his fists and dodging about in the garden. He stopped then, and coughed, and set his panama straight, and avoided our eyes, and turned his back and walked slowly to the deck chair.

We both threw gravel at him.

'I'll give him "Come on!" ' the boy said, as we ran along the playground away from the shouts of Mr. Samuels and down the steps on to the hill.

We walked home together. I admired his bloody nose. He said that my eye was like a poached egg, only black.

'I've never seen such a lot of blood,' I said.

He said I had the best black eye in Wales, perhaps it was the best black eye in Europe; he bet Tunney never had a black eye like that.

'And there's blood all over your shirt.'

'Sometimes I bleed in dollops,' he said.

On Walter's Road we passed a group of high school girls, and I cocked my cap and hoped my eye was as big as a bluebag, and he walked with his coat flung open to show the bloodstains.

I was a hooligan all during dinner, and a bully, and as bad as a boy from the Sandbanks, and I should have more respect, and I sat silently, like Tunney, over the sago pudding. That afternoon I went to school with an eye-shade on. If I had had a black silk sling I would have been as gay and desperate as the wounded captain in the book that my sister used to read, and that I read under the bedclothes at night, secretly with a flash-lamp.

On the road, a boy from an inferior school, where the parents did not have to pay anything, called me, 'One eye!' in a harsh, adult voice. I took no notice, but walked along whistling, my good eye on the summer clouds sailing, beyond insult, above Terrace Road.

The mathematics master said, 'I see that Mr. Thomas at the back of the class has been straining his eyesight. But it isn't over his homework, is it, gentlemen?'

Gilbert Rees, next to me, laughed loudest.

'I'll break your leg after school!' I said.

He'd hobble, howling, up to the head master's study. A deep hush in the school. A message on a plate brought by the porter. 'The head master's compliments, sir, and will you come at once?' 'How did you happen to break this boy's leg?' 'Oh? Damn and bottom, the agony!' cried Gilbert Rees. 'Just a little twist,' I would say. 'I don't know my own strength. I apologize. But there's nothing to worry about. Let me set the leg, sir.' A rapid manipulation, the click of a bone. 'Doctor Thomas, sir, at your service.' Mrs. Rees was on her knees. 'How can I thank you?' 'It's nothing at all, dear lady. Wash his ears every morning. Throw away his rulers. Pour his red and green inks down the sink.'

In Mr. Trotter's drawing class we drew naked girls inaccurately on sheets of paper under our drawings of a vase and passed them along under the desks. Some of the drawings were detailed strangely, others were tailed off like mermaids. Gilbert Rees drew the vase only.

'Sleep with your wife, sir?'

'What did you say?'

'Lend me a knife, sir?'

'What would you do if you had a million pounds?'

'I'd buy a Bugatti and a Rolls and a Bentley and I'd go two hundred miles an hour on Pendine sands.'

'I'd buy a harem and keep the girls in the gym.'

'I'd buy a house like Mrs. Cotmore-Richard's, twice as big as hers, and a cricket field and a football field and a proper garage with mechanics and a lift.'

'And a lavatory as big as, as big as the Melba pavilion, with plush seats and golden chains and . . .'

'And I'd smoke cigarettes with real gold tips, better than Morris's Blue Book.'

'I'd buy all the railway trains, and only 4A could travel in them.'

'And not Gilbert Rees either.'

'What's the longest you've been?'

'I went to Edinburgh.'

'My father went to Salonika in the War.'

'Where's that, Cyril?'

'Cyril, tell us about Mrs. Pussie Edwards in Hanover Street.'

'Well, my brother says he can do anything.'

I drew a wild guess below the waist, and wrote Pussie Edwards in small letters at the foot of the page.

'Cave!'

'Hide your drawings.'

'I bet you a greyhound can go faster than a horse.'

Everybody liked the drawing class, except Mr. Trotter.

In the evening, before calling on my new friend, I sat in my bedroom by the boiler and read through my exercise-books full of poems. There were Danger Don'ts on the backs. On my bedroom walls were pictures of Shakespeare, Walter de la Mare torn from my father's Christmas *Bookman*, Robert Browning, Stacy Aumonier, Rupert Brooke, a bearded man who I had discovered was Whittier, Watts's 'Hope', and a Sunday school certificate I was ashamed to want to pull down. A poem I had had printed in the 'Wales Day by Day' column of the *Western Mail* was pasted on the mirror to make me blush, but the shame of the poem had died. Across the poem I had written, with a stolen quill and in flourishes, 'Homer Nods.' I was always waiting for the opportunity to bring someone into my bedroom—'Come into my den; excuse the untidiness; take a chair. No! Not that one, it's broken!'—and force him to see the poem accidentally. 'I put it there to make me blush.' But nobody ever came in except my mother.

Walking to his house in the early dusk through solid, deserted professional avenues lined with trees, I recited pieces of my poems and heard my voice, like a stranger's voice in Park Drive accompanied by the tap-tapping of nailed boots, rise very thinly up through the respectable autumn evening.

> 'My mind is fashioned
> In the ways of intertissue;
> Veiled and passioned
> Are the thoughts that issue
> From its well of furtive lust
> Raptured by the devil's dust.'

If I looked through a window on to the road, I would see a scarlet-capped boy with big boots striding down the middle, and would wonder who it could be. If I were a young girl watching, my face like Mona Lisa's, my coal-black hair coiled in earphones, I'd see beneath the 'Boys' Department' suit a manly body with hair and sun tan, and call him and ask, 'Will you have tea or cocktails?' and hear his voice reciting the *Grass Blade's Psalm* in the half-dark of the heavily curtained and coloured drawing-room hung about with famous reproductions and glowing with books and wine bottles,

'The frost has lain,
Frost that is dark with flowered slain,
Fragilely strewn
With patches of illuminated moon,
About my lonely head in flagged unlovely red,

'The frost has spake,
Frost secretive and thrilled in silent flake,
With unseen lips of blue
Glass in the glaze stars threw,
Only to my ears, has spake in visionary tears.

'The frost has known,
From scattered conclave by the few winds
    blown,
That the lone genius in my roots,
Bare down there in a jungle of fruits,
Has planted a green year, for praise in the heart
of my upgrowing days.

'The frost has filled
My heart with longing that night's sleeve spilled,
Frost of celestial vapour fraught,
Frost that the columns of unfallen snow have sought,
With desire for the fields of space hovering about my
    single place.'

'Look! There's a strange boy, walking alone like a prince.'

'No, no, like a wolf! Look at his long stride!' Sketty church was shaking its bells for me.

> 'When I am strewn low
> And all my ashes are
> Dust in a dumb provoking show
> Of minatory star . . .'

I recited. A young man and woman, arm in arm, suddenly appeared from a black lane between houses. I changed my recitation into a tune and hummed past them. They would be tittering together now, with their horrid bodies close. Cissy, moony, long hair. I whistled hard and loud, kicked a tradesmen's entrance, and glanced back over my shoulder. The couple were gone. Here's a kick at 'The Elms'. 'Where are the bleedy elms, mister?' Here's a handful of gravel, Mrs. 'The Croft', right at your window. One night I would paint 'Bum' all over the front gate of 'Kia-ora'.

A woman stood on 'Lyndhurst' steps with a hissing pom, and, stuffing my cap in my pocket, I was off down the road; and there was Dan's house, 'Warmley', with music coming loudly out of it.

He was a composer and a poet too; he had written seven historical novels before he was twelve, and he played the piano and the violin; his mother made wool pictures, his brother was a clerk at the docks and syncopated, his aunt kept a preparatory school on the first floor, and his father wrote music for the organ. All this he had told me as we walked home bleeding, strutting by the gym-frocks waving to boys in the trams.

My new friend's mother answered the door with a ball of wool in her hand. Dan, in the upstairs drawing-room, heard my arrival and played the piano faster.

'I didn't hear you come in,' he said when I found him. He finished on a grand chord, stretching all his fingers.

The room was splendidly untidy, full of wool and paper and open cupboards stacked with things you could never find; all the expensive furniture had been kicked; a waistcoat hung on the chandelier. I thought I could live for ever in that room, writing and fighting and spilling ink, having my friends for picnics there after midnight with Walker's rum-and-butter and charlottes russes from Eynon's, and Cydrax and Vino.

He showed me his books and his seven novels. All the novels were about battles, sieges, and kings. 'Just early stuff,' he said.

He let me take out his violin and make a cat noise.

We sat on a sofa in the window and talked as though we had always known each other. Would the 'Swans' beat the 'Spurs'? When could girls have babies? Was Arnott's average last year better than Clay's?

'That's my father outside there on the road,' he said, 'the tall one waving his arms.'

Two men were talking on the tram lines. Mr. Jenkyn looked as if he were trying to swim down Eversley Road, he breast-stroked the air and beat on the ground with his feet, and then he limped and raised one shoulder higher than the other.

'Perhaps he's describing a fight,' I said.

'Or telling Mr. Morris a story about cripples,' said Dan. 'Can you play the piano?'

'I can do chords, but not tunes,' I said.

We played a duet with crossed hands.

'Now who's that sonata by?'

We made a Dr. Percy, who was the greatest composer for four hands in the world, and I was Paul America, the pianist, and Dan was Winter Vaux.

I read him an exercise-book full of poems. He listened wisely, like a boy aged a hundred, his head on one side and his spectacles shaking on his swollen nose. 'This is called *Warp*,' I said,

> 'Like suns red from running tears,
> Five suns in the glass,
> Together, separate yet, yet separately round,
> Red perhaps, but the glass is as pale as grass,
> Glide, without sound.
> In unity, five tears lid-awake, suns yet, but salt,
> Five inscrutable spears in the head,
> Each sun but an agony,
> Twist perhaps, pain bled of hate,
> Five into one, the one made of five into one, early
> Suns distorted to late.
> All of them now, madly and desolate,
> Spun with the cloth of the five, run
> Widely and foaming, wildly and desolate,
> Shoot through and dive. One of the five is the sun.'

The noise of the trams past the house clattered away as far as the sea or farther, into the dredgered bay. Nobody had ever listened like that before. The school had vanished, leaving on Mount Pleasant hill a deep hole that smelt of cloakrooms and locker mice, and 'Warmley' shone in the dark of a town I did not know. In the still room, that had never been strange to me, sitting in heaps of coloured wool, swollen-nosed and one-eyed, we acknowledged our gifts. The future spread out beyond the window, over Singleton Park crowded with lovers messing about, and into smoky London paved with poems.

Mrs. Jenkyn peered round the door and switched the light on. 'There, that's more homely,' she said. 'You aren't cats.'

The future went out with the light, and we played a thumping piece by Dr. Percy—'Have you ever heard anything so beautiful? Louder, louder, America!' said Dan. 'Leave a bit of bass for me,' I said—until the next-door wall was rapped.

'That's the Careys. Mr. Carey's a Cape Horner,' Dan said.

We played him one harsh, whaling piece before Mrs. Jenkyn, with wool and needles, ran upstairs.

When she had gone, Dan said, 'Why is a man always ashamed of his mother?'

'Perhaps he isn't when he is older,' I said, but I doubted it. The week before I was walking down High Street with three boys after school, and I saw my mother with a Mrs. Partridge outside the Kardomah. I knew she would stop me in front of the others and say, 'Now you be home early for tea,' and I wanted High Street to open and suck me down. I loved her and disowned her. 'Let's cross over,' I said, 'there's some sailor's boots in Griffith's window.' But there was only a dummy with a golf suit on, and a roll of tweed.

'Supper isn't for half an hour yet. What shall we do?'

'Let's see who can hold up that chair the longest,' I said.

'No, let's edit a paper: you do the literature, I'll do the music.'

'What shall we call it, then?'

He wrote, 'The———, edited by D. Jenkyn and D. Thomas,' on the back of a hat-box from under the sofa. The rhythm was better with D. Thomas and D. Jenkyn, but it was his house.

'What about *The Maestersingers?*'

'No, that's too musical,' I said.

'*The Warmley Magazine?*'

'No,' I said, 'I live in "Glanrhyd".'

After the hat-box was covered, we wrote, '*The Thunderer*, edited by D. Jenkyn/Thomas' in chalk on a piece of cardboard and pinned it on the wall.

'Would you like to see our maid's bedroom?' asked Dan. We whispered up to the attic.

'What's her name?'

'Hilda.'

'Is she young?'

'No, she's twenty or thirty.'

Her bed was untidy. 'My mother says you can always smell a maid.' We smelled the sheets. 'I can't smell anything.'

In her brass-bound box was a framed photograph of a young man wearing plus-fours.

'That's her boy.'

'Let's give him a moustache.'

Somebody moved downstairs, a voice called, 'Supper now!' and we hurried out, leaving the box open. 'One night we'll hide under her bed,' Dan said as we opened the dining-room door.

Mr. Jenkyn, Mrs. Jenkyn, Dan's aunt, and a Reverend Bevan and Mrs. Bevan were seated at the table.

Mr. Bevan said grace. When he stood up, it was just as though he were still sitting down, he was so short. 'Bless our repast this evening,' he said, as though he didn't like the food at all. But once 'Amen' was over, he went at the cold meat like a dog.

Mrs. Bevan didn't look all there. She stared at the table-cloth and made hesitant movements with her knife and fork. She appeared to be wondering which to cut up first, the meat or the cloth.

Dan and I stared at her with delight; he kicked me under the table and I spilt the salt. In the commotion I managed to put some vinegar on his bread.

Mrs. Jenkyn said, while everyone except Mr. Bevan was watching Mrs. Bevan moving her knife slowly along the edge of her plate, 'I do hope you like cold lamb.'

Mrs. Bevan smiled at her, assured, and began to eat. She was grey-haired and grey-faced. Perhaps she was grey all over. I tried to undress her, but my mind grew frightened when it came to her short flannel petticoat and navy bloomers to the knees. I couldn't even dare unbutton her tall boots to see how grey her legs were. She looked up from her plate and gave me a wicked smile.

Blushing, I turned to answer Mr. Jenkyn, who was asking me how old I was. I told him, but added one year. Why did I lie then? I wondered. If I lost my cap and found it in my bedroom, and my mother asked me where I had found it, I would say, 'In the attic,' or 'Under the hall-stand.' It was exciting to have to keep wary all the time in case I contradicted myself, to make up the story of a film I pretended to have seen and put Jack Holt in Richard Dix's place.

'Fifteen and three-quarters,' said Mr. Jenkyn, 'that's a very exact age. I see we have a mathematician with us. Now see if he can do this little sum.'

He finished his supper and laid out matches on the plate.

'That's an old one, Dad,' Dan said.

'Oh, I'd like to see it very much,' I said in my best voice. I wanted to come to the house again. This was better than home, and there was a woman off her head, too.

When I failed to place the matches rightly, Mr. Jenkyn showed me how it was done, and, still not understanding, I thanked him and asked him for another one. It was almost as good being a hypocrite as being a liar; it made you warm and shameful.

'What were you talking to Mr. Morris about in the street, Dad?' asked Dan. 'We saw you from upstairs.'

'I was telling him how the Swansea and District Male Voice did the *Messiah*, that's all. Why do you ask?'

Mr. Bevan couldn't eat any more, he was full. For the first time since supper began, he looked round the table. He didn't seem to like what he saw. 'How are studies progressing, Daniel?'

'Listen to Mr. Bevan, Dan, he's asking you a question.'

'Oh, so so.'

'So so?'

'I mean they're going very well, thank you, Mr. Bevan.'

'Young people should attempt to say what they mean.'

Mrs. Bevan giggled, and asked for more meat. 'More meat,' she said.

'And you, young man, have you a mathematical bent?'

'No, sir,' I said, 'I like English.'

'He's a poet,' said Dan, and looked uncomfortable.

'A brother poet,' Mr. Bevan corrected, showing his teeth.

'Mr. Bevan has published books,' said Mr. Jenkyn. '*Proserpine, Psyche*——'

'*Orpheus*,' said Mr. Bevan sharply.

'And *Orpheus*. You must show Mr. Bevan some of your verses.'

'I haven't got anything with me, Mr. Jenkyn.'

'A poet,' said Mr. Bevan, 'should carry his verses in his head.'

'I remember them all right,' I said.

'Recite me your latest one; I'm always very interested.'

'What a gathering,' Mrs. Jenkyn said, 'poets, musicians, preachers. We only want a painter now, don't we?'

'I don't think you'll like the very latest one,' I said.

'Perhaps,' said Mr. Bevan, smiling, 'I am the best judge of that.'

'Frivolous is my hate,' I said, wanting to die, watching Mr. Bevan's teeth,

> 'Singed with bestial remorse
> Of unfulfilment of desired force,
> And lust of tearing hate;
>
> 'Now could I raise
> Her dead, dark body to my own
> And hear the joyous rustle of her bone
> And in her eyes see deathly blaze;
>
> 'Now could I wake
> To passion after death, and taste
> The rapture of her hating, tear and waste
> Of body. Break, her dead, dark body, break.'

105

Dan kicked my shins in the silence before Mr. Bevan said, 'The influence is obvious, of course. "Break, break, break, on thy cold, grey stones, O sea." '

'Hubert knows Tennyson backwards,' said Mrs. Bevan, 'backwards.'

'Can we go upstairs now?' Dan asked.

'No annoying Mr. Carey then.'

And we shut the door softly behind us and ran upstairs with our hands over our mouths.

'Damn! Damn! Damn!' said Dan. 'Did you see the reverend's face?'

We imitated him up and down the room, and had a short fight on the carpet. Dan's nose began to bleed again. 'That's nothing, it'll stop in a minute. I can bleed when I like.'

'Tell me about Mrs. Bevan. Is she mad?'

'She's terribly mad, she doesn't know who she is. She tried to throw herself out of the window but he didn't take any notice, so she came up to our house and told mother all about it.'

Mrs. Bevan knocked and walked in. 'I hope I'm not interrupting you.'

'No, of course not, Mrs. Bevan.'

'I wanted a little change of air,' she said. She sat down in the wool on the sofa by the window.

'Isn't it a close night?' said Dan. 'Would you like the window open?'

She looked at the window.

'I can easily open it for you,' Dan said, and winked at me.

'Let me open it for you, Mrs. Bevan,' I said.

'It's good to have the window open.'

'And this is a nice high window too.'

'Plenty of air from the sea.'

'Let it be dear,' she said. 'I'll just sit here and wait for my husband.'

She played with the balls of wool, picked up a needle and tapped it gently on the palm of her hand.

'Is Mr. Bevan going to be long?'

'I'll just sit and wait for my husband,' she said.

We talked to her some more about windows, but she only smiled and undid the wool, and once she put the blunt end of the long needle in her ear. Soon we grew tired of watching her, and Dan played the piano—'My twentieth sonata,' he said, 'this one is *Homage to Beethoven*'—and at half-past nine I had to go home.

I said goodnight to Mrs. Bevan, who waved the needle and bowed sitting down, and Mr. Bevan downstairs gave me his cold hand to shake, and Mr. and Mrs. Jenkyn told me to come again, and the quiet aunt gave me a Mars bar.

'I'll send you a bit of the way,' said Dan.

Outside, on the pavement, in the warm night, we looked up at the lighted drawing-room window. It was the only light in the road.

'Look! There she is!'

Mrs. Bevan's face was pressed against the glass, her hook nose flattened, her lips pressed tight, and we ran all the way down Eversley Road in case she jumped.

At the corner, Dan said, 'I must leave you now, I've got to finish a string trio tonight.'

'I'm working on a long poem,' I said, 'about the princes of Wales and the wizards and everybody.'

We both went home to bed.

A Child's Christmas
in Wales

One Christmas was so much like another, in those years around the sea-town corner now and out of all sound except the distant speaking of the voices I sometimes hear a moment before sleep, that I can never remember whether it snowed for six days and six nights when I was twelve or whether is snowed for twelve days and twelve nights when I was six.

All the Christmases roll down toward the two-tongued sea, like a cold and headlong moon bundling down the sky that was our street; and they stop at the rim of the ice-edged, fish-freezing waves, and I plunge my hands in the snow and bring out whatever I can find. In goes my hand into that wool-white bell-tongued ball of holidays resting at the rim of the carol-singing sea, and out come Mrs. Prothero and the firemen.

It was on the afternoon of the day of Christmas Eve, and I was in Mrs. Prothero's garden, waiting for cats, with her son Jim. It was snowing. It was always snowing at Christmas. December, in my memory, is white as Lapland, though there were no reindeers. But there were cats. Patient, cold and callous, our hands wrapped in socks, we waited to snowball the cats. Sleek and long as jaguars and horrible-whiskered, spitting and snarling, they would slink and sidle over the white back-garden walls, and the lynx-eyed hunters, Jim and I, fur-capped and moccasined trappers from Hudson Bay, off Mumbles Road, would hurl our deadly snowballs at the green of their eyes.

The wise cats never appeared. We were so still, Eskimo-footed arctic marksmen in the muffling silence of the eternal snows—eternal, ever since Wednesday—that we never heard Mrs. Prothero's first cry from her igloo at the bottom of the garden. Or, if we heard it at all, it was, to us, like the far-off challenge of our enemy and prey, the neighbour's polar cat. But soon the voice grew louder. 'Fire!' cried Mrs. Prothero, and she beat the dinner-gong.

And we ran down the garden, with the snowballs in our arms, toward the house; and smoke, indeed, was pouring out of the dining-room, and the gong was bombilating, and Mrs. Prothero was announcing ruin like a town crier in Pompeii. This was better than all the cats in Wales standing on the wall in a row. We bounded into the house, laden with snowballs, and stopped at the open door of the smoke-filled room.

Something was burning all right; perhaps it was Mr. Prothero, who always slept there after midday dinner with a newspaper over his face. But he was standing in the middle of the room, saying, 'A fine Christmas!' and smacking at the smoke with a slipper. 'Call the fire brigade,' cried Mrs. Prothero as she beat the gong.

'They won't be there,' said Mr. Prothero, 'it's Christmas.'

There was no fire to be seen, only clouds of smoke and Mr. Prothero, standing in the middle of them, waving his slipper as though he were conducting.

'Do something,' he said.

110

And we threw all our snowballs into the smoke—I think we missed Mr. Prothero—and ran out of the house to the telephone box.

'Let's call the police as well,' Jim said.

'And the ambulance.'

'And Ernie Jenkins, he likes fires.'

But we only called the fire brigade, and soon the fire engine came and three tall men in helmets brought a hose into the house and Mr. Prothero got out just in time before they turned it on. Nobody could have had a noisier Christmas Eve. And when the firemen turned off the hose and were standing in the wet, smoky room, Jim's aunt, Miss Prothero, came downstairs and peered in at them. Jim and I waited, very quietly, to hear what she would say to them. She said the right thing, always. She looked at the three tall firemen in their shining helmets, standing among the smoke and cinders and dissolving snowballs, and she said, 'Would you like anything to read?'

Years and years and years ago, when I was a boy, when there were wolves in Wales, and birds the colour of red-flannel petticoats whisked past the harp-shaped hills, when we sang and wallowed all night and day in caves that smelt like Sunday afternoons in damp front farmhouse parlours, and we chased, with the jawbones of deacons, the English and the bears, before the motor car, before the wheel, before the duchess-faced horse, when we rode the daft and happy hills bareback, it snowed and it snowed. But here a small boy says, 'It snowed last year, too. I made a snowman and my brother knocked it down and I knocked my brother down and then we had tea.'

'But that was not the same snow,' I say. 'Our snow was

111

not only shaken from whitewash buckets down the sky, it came shawling out of the ground and swam and drifted out of the arms and hands and bodies of the trees; snow grew overnight on the roofs of the houses like a pure and grandfather moss, minutely white-ivied the walls and settled on the postman, opening the gate, like a dumb, numb thunderstorm of white, torn Christmas cards.'

'Were there postmen then, too?'

'With sprinkling eyes and wind-cherried noses, on spread, frozen feet they crunched up to the doors and mittened on them manfully. But all that the children could hear was a ringing of bells.'

'You mean that the postman went rat-a-tat-tat and the doors rang?'

'I mean that the bells that the children could hear were inside them.'

'I only hear thunder sometimes, never bells.'

'There were church bells, too.'

'Inside them?'

'No, no, no, in the bat-black, snow-white belfries, tugged by bishops and storks. And they rang their tidings over the bandaged town, over the frozen foam of the powder and ice-cream hills, over the crackling sea. It seemed that all the churches boomed for joy under my window; and the weathercocks crew for Christmas, on our fence.'

'Get back to the postmen.'

'They were just ordinary postmen, fond of walking and dogs and Christmas and the snow. They knocked on the doors with blue knuckles . . .'

'Ours has got a black knocker . . .'

'And then they stood on the white Welcome mat in the

little, drifted porches and huffed and puffed, making ghosts with their breath, and jogged from foot to foot like small boys wanting to go out.'

'And then the Presents?'

'And then the Presents, after the Christmas box. And the cold postman, with a rose on his button-nose, tingled down the tea-tray-slithered run of the chilly glinting hill. He went in his ice-bound boots like a man on fish-monger's slabs. He wagged his bag like a frozen camel's hump, dizzily turned the corner on one foot, and, by God, he was gone.'

'Get back to the Presents.'

'There were the Useful Presents: engulfing mufflers of the old coach days, and mittens made for giant sloths; zebra scarfs of a substance like silky gum that could be tug-o'-warred down to the galoshes; blinding tam-o'-shanters like patchwork tea cosies and bunny-suited bus-bies and balaclavas for victims of head-shrinking tribes; from aunts who always wore wool next to the skin there were moustached and rasping vests that made you won-der why the aunts had any skin left at all; and once I had a little crocheted nose bag from an aunt now, alas, no longer whinnying with us. And pictureless books in which small boys, though warned with quotations not to, *would* skate on Farmer Giles' pond and did and drowned; and books that told me everything about the wasp, except why.'

'Go on to the Useless Presents.'

'Bags of moist and many-coloured jelly babies and a folded flag and a false nose and a tram-conductor's cap and a machine that punched tickets and rang a bell; never a catapult; once, by mistake that no one could explain, a little hatchet; and a celluloid duck that made, when you pressed it, a most unducklike sound, a mewing moo that an ambitious cat might make who wished to be a cow; and a painting book in which I could make the grass, the trees, the sea and the animals any colour I pleased, and still the dazzling sky-blue sheep are grazing in the red field under the rainbow-billed and pea-green birds.

'Hardboileds, toffee, fudge and allsorts, crunches, cracknels, humbugs, glaciers, marzipan, and butterwelsh for the Welsh. And troops of bright tin soldiers who, if they could not fight, could always run. And Snakes-and-Families and Happy Ladders. And Easy Hobbi-Games for Little Engineers, complete with instructions.

'Oh, easy for Leonardo! And a whistle to make the dogs bark to wake up the old man next door to make him beat on the wall with his stick to shake our picture off the wall.

'And a packet of cigarettes: you put one in your mouth and you stood at the corner of the street and you waited for hours, in vain, for an old lady to scold you for smoking a cigarette, and then with a smirk you ate it. And then it was breakfast under the balloons.'

'Were there Uncles like in our house?'

'There are always Uncles at Christmas.

'The same Uncles. And on Christmas mornings, with dog-disturbing whistle and sugar fags, I would scour the swatched town for the news of the little world, and find always a dead bird by the white Post Office or by the deserted swings; perhaps a robin, all but one of his fires out. Men and women wading or scooping back from chapel, with taproom noses and wind-bussed cheeks, all albinos, huddled their stiff black jarring feathers against the irreligious snow.

'Mistletoe hung from the gas brackets in all the front parlours; there was sherry and walnuts and bottled beer and crackers by the dessertspoon; and cats in their fur-abouts watched the fires; and the high-heaped fire spat, all ready for the chestnuts and the mulling pokers.

'Some few large men sat in the front parlours, without their collars, Uncles almost certainly, trying their new cigars, holding them out judiciously at arms' length, returning them to their mouths, coughing, then holding them out again as though waiting for the explosion; and some few small Aunts, not wanted in the kitchen, nor anywhere else for that matter, sat on the very edges of their chairs, poised and brittle, afraid to break, like faded cups and saucers.'

Not many those mornings trod the piling streets; an old man always, fawn-bowlered, yellow-gloved and, at this time of year, with spats of snow, would take his constitutional to the white bowling green and back, as he would take it wet or fine on Christmas Day or Dooms-day; sometimes two hale young men, with big pipes blazing, no overcoats and wind-blown scarfs, would trudge, unspeaking, down to the forlorn sea, to work up an appetite, to blow away the fumes, who knows, to walk into the waves until nothing of them was left but the two curling smoke clouds of their inextinguishable briars. Then I would be slap-dashing home, the gravy smell of the dinners of others, the bird smell, the brandy, the pudding and mince, coiling up to my nostrils, when out of a snow-clogged side lane would come a boy the spit of myself, with a pink-tipped cigarette and the violet past of a black eye, cocky as a bullfinch, leering all to himself.

I hated him on sight and sound, and would be about to

put my dog-whistle to my lips and blow him off the face of Christmas when suddenly he, with a violet wink, put *his* whistle to *his* lips and blew so stridently, so high, so exquisitely loud, that gobbling faces, their cheeks bulged with goose, would press against their tinselled windows, the whole length of the white echoing street. For dinner we had turkey and blazing pudding, and after dinner the Uncles sat in front of the fire, loosened all buttons, put their large moist hands over their watch chains, groaned a little and slept. Mothers, aunts and sisters scuttled to and fro, bearing tureens. Auntie Bessie, who had already been frightened, twice, by a clock-work mouse, whimpered at the sideboard and had some elderberry wine. The dog was sick. Auntie Dosie had to have three aspirins, but Auntie Hannah, who liked port, stood in the middle of the snowbound back yard, singing like a big-bosomed thrush. I would blow up balloons to see how big they would blow up to; and, when they burst, which they all did, the Uncles jumped and rumbled. In the rich and heavy afternoon, the Uncles breathing like dolphins and the snow descending, I would sit among festoons and Chinese lanterns and nibble dates and try to make a model man-o'-war, following the Instructions for Little Engineers, and produce what might be mistaken for a sea-going tramcar.

Or I would go out, my bright new boots squeaking, into the white world, on to the seaward hill, to call on Jim and Dan and Jack and to pad through the still streets, leaving huge deep footprints on the hidden pavements.

'I bet people will think there's been hippos.'

'What would you do if you saw a hippo coming down our street?'

'I'd go like this, bang! I'd throw him over the railings and roll him down the hill and then I'd tickle him under the ear and he'd wag his tail.'

'What would you do if you saw *two* hippos?'

Iron-flanked and bellowing he-hippos clanked and battered through the scudding snow toward us as we passed Mr. Daniel's house.

'Let's post Mr. Daniel a snowball through his letter-box.'

'Let's write things in the snow.'

'Let's write, "Mr. Daniel looks like a spaniel" all over his lawn.'

Or we walked on the white shore.

'Can the fishes see it's snowing?'

The silent one-clouded heavens drifted on to the sea. Now we were snow-blind travellers lost on the north hills, and vast dewlapped dogs, with flasks round their necks, ambled and shambled up to us, baying, 'Excelsior'. We returned home through the poor streets where only a few children fumbled with bare red fingers in the wheel-rutted snow and cat-called after us, their voices fading away, as we trudged uphill, into the cries of the dock birds and the hooting of ships out in the whirling bay. And then, at tea the recovered Uncles would be jolly; and the ice cake loomed in the centre of the table like a marble grave. Auntie Hannah laced her tea with rum, because it was only once a year.

Bring out the tall tales now that we told by the fire as the gaslight bubbled like a diver. Ghosts whooed like owls in the long nights when I dared not look over my shoulder; animals lurked in the cubbyhole under the stairs where the gas meter ticked. And I remember that

119

we went singing carols once, when there wasn't the shaving of a moon to light the flying streets. At the end of a long road was a drive that led to a large house, and we stumbled up the darkness of the drive that night, each one of us afraid, each one holding a stone in his hand in case, and all of us too brave to say a word. The wind through the trees made noises as of old and unpleasant and maybe web-footed men wheezing in caves. We reached the black bulk of the house.

'What shall we give them? *Hark the Herald*?'

'No,' Jack said, '*Good King Wenceslas*. I'll count three.'

One, two, three, and we began to sing, our voices high and seemingly distant in the snow-felted darkness round the house that was occupied by nobody we knew. We stood close together, near the dark door.

> Good King Wenceslas looked out
> On the Feast of Stephen . . .

And then a small, dry voice, like the voice of someone who has not spoken for a long time, joined our singing: a small, dry, eggshell voice from the other side of the door: a small dry voice through the keyhole. And when we stopped running we were outside *our* house; the front room was lovely; balloons floated under the hot-water-bottle-gulping gas; everything was good again and shone over the town.

'Perhaps it was a ghost,' Jim said.

'Perhaps it was trolls,' Dan said, who was always reading.

'Let's go in and see if there's any jelly left,' Jack said. And we did that.

Always on Christmas night there was music. An uncle played the fiddle, a cousin sang *Cherry Ripe*, and another uncle sang *Drake's Drum*. It was very warm in the little house.

Auntie Hannah, who had got on to the parsnip wine, sang a song about Bleeding Hearts and Death, and then another in which she said her heart was like a Bird's Nest; and then everybody laughed again; and then I went to bed. Looking through my bedroom window, out into the moonlight and the unending smoke-coloured snow, I could see the lights in the windows of all the other houses on our hill and hear the music rising from them up the long, steadily falling night. I turned the gas down, I got into bed. I said some words to the close and holy darkness, and then I slept.